SUSPECT

VOLUME 1, YEAR 1
(FEBRUARY 2022–JANUARY 2023)

SUSPECT

Editor-in-Chief: Jee Leong Koh

Essay: Jerrine Tan, Prasanthi Ram,
and Alysha Chandra

Fiction: Sharmini Aphrodite

Poetry: Marylyn Tan

Interview: Jade Onn and Janelle Tan

Review: Maggie Wang
and Miranda Jeyaretnam

Art: Miki Wang

Web: Emily von Borstel

With Assistant Editor, Gaudy Boy:
Isabel Drake

CONTENTS

Author

SUSPECT

VOLUME 1, YEAR 1
(FEBRUARY 2022–JANUARY 2023)

EDITOR'S INTRODUCTION

SUSPECT, as in "we suspect this work has qualities of greatness." As in looking from the ground up, and not top down. As in "incredulity towards metanarratives" (Lyotard) in favor of microhistories, subversive perspectives, and marginalized identities. As in an online journal of Asian writing and art, published by the New York City-based literary nonprofit Singapore Unbound/ indie press Gaudy Boy. As in a print selection celebrating the first year of publication.

Launched on February 22, 2022, SUSPECT has had a tremendous start, thanks to gifted and courageous contributors who trusted us with their writing and art. When Kazakhstani writers spoke out against the brutal crackdown on dissent in their country, we were honored to publish the Russian originals and English translations of protest writings by six poets. Other published translations include poems in Bhojpuri, an Indian language still fighting for complete recognition as distinct from Hindi, and poems in Farsi by the free-verse pioneer Nima Youshij.

Since English is an Asian language too, we are pleased to publish original works in English, alongside translations. Contributors come from all over the world, including Bangladesh, Canada, China, India, Israel, Malaysia, Singapore, the Philippines, South Korea, the UK, and the US. In fact, it is more accurate to say that there are as many Englishes as there are Asias. We try to keep this fact in view by maintaining the contributors' English as part of our editorial policy, instead of standardizing it according to the British or American variant.

These English-language works span many topics and perspectives, and some of them broach taboo subjects, such as sexual enslavement during World War II and a sister's suicide. In considering these difficult topics, we have steered clear of glamorizing them for mass consumption, in favor of—a paradox—an artful honesty. It is art that brings writer and reader together to examine honestly what we would rather not. In the case of child abuse and marriage in Bangladesh, we learned to give more weight to exposing a social evil in the writer's country than to privileging social squeamishness in more advanced capitalist societies.

In our book reviews, a sample of which is also given in this print anthology, we look critically at important works by writers who should be better known. We offer context and opinion. We ask our reviewers for precise yet graceful writing. We aim to enable the discovery of Asian writers who speak authentically, and not merely commercially, about their part of the world and about their part in the world.

If you like what you read in this anthology, please consider submitting your unpublished work to us. As you see, our definition of Asia and Asian is broad and multiple. We pay our contributors. If you believe in the power of literature to shift perspective, deepen understanding, and imagine alternatives, make a generous donation to our work at: https://fundraising.fracturedatlas .org/singapore-unbound. Together we will grow SUSPECT beyond its promising first year to be a force for change.

Yours suspiciously,
Jee Leong Koh
Editor-in-Chief

"FOG OF JANUARY,"
"[UNTITLED] 'AN INHABITANT OF THE OUTSKIRTS',"
"DON'T SHOOT,"
"THIS IS THEM SHOOTING AT ME," "LULLABY,"
"[UNTITLED] 'AND IT'S SCARY, LORD, IT'S SCARY—',"
"[UNTITLED] 'THIS CITY'S IMMORTALIZED'"

Oral Arukenova, Anastasiya Belousova, Asel Omar,
Kanat Omar, Ramil Niyazov, and Irina Gumyrkina

Translated by Shelley Fairweather-Vega and Katherine E. Young

Translators' Statement

In early January 2022, Central Asia was rocked by the bloody aftermath of unexpected protests in Kazakhstan. Those protests started out peacefully but soon turned chaotic, with official announcements that unspecified "terrorists" had invaded the country in an attempt to topple the government, and orders were issued to shoot to kill. Soldiers imported from Russia appeared in the streets. Protesters dispersed quickly in half a dozen cities, but in Almaty, the cultural capital, the chaos grew worse. Over the course of several foggy January days, the time usually dedicated to celebrating the New Year devolved into a nightmare. Innocent people of all ethnicities, young and old, were shot where they stood or were arrested and disappeared. As of more than a month later, no list of the dead and injured and arrested had yet been made available, and nobody was even sure how many people were dead or missing.

Translators Shelley Fairweather-Vega and Katherine E. Young spent three weeks assembling and translating seven poems by half a dozen Kazakhstani poets who reflect on this trauma and uncertainty in the immediate aftermath of events. Most of these poems appeared in the online literary journal *Litterratura* in February 2022, while others first appeared on Facebook. Our selections were driven purely by how these poems resonated with us personally. Given unlimited time and emotional capacity, we would have translated even more. While all these poems were originally written in the Russian language, each is suffused with a decidedly Kazakhstani mentality. Together, they are a plea for understanding, for answers, for a better future for their country and their compatriots.

We should note that as we worked on these translations, Russian troops were massing on the border of Ukraine, another country trying hard to determine its own fate. While still processing their own trauma, our Kazakhstani friends have also been speaking out boldly against Russian aggression in Ukraine—including by public protests!—despite the fact that the Kazakh government officially professes neutrality. Their principled stand and personal bravery are examples for us all.

ТУМАННЫЙ ЯНВАРЬ

Орал Арукенова

мама говорила

нет ничего прекраснее слова

ужаснее слова

папа говорил

нет ничего важнее истины

страшнее истины

внутренняя волчица шепчет

нет ничего сильнее крови

беззащитнее крова

я говорю себе не бойся

это всего лишь слова—

истина дом кровь

туманный январь

в сером небе ни звезд ни луны

лишь отблески взрывов

на стеклах высотки

весь мир растворился

в дыме и хаосе.

прикрываясь туманом

из верхних престижных

стекались к центру

бородатые рослые

призраки прошлого—

ассасины

из нижних районов

шли толпы разгневанных

оседлать

нефте-долларового быка

выхлестнуть ярость

на гламурные символы

хозяев жизни и слуг народа.

жители города яблок

не сразу поняли разницу

между хлопками петард

и стрельбой автомата

из окон домов

несмелыми струйками

сквозь грохот и гарь

пробивались молитвы

утренние вечерние

многократные

пятничные

субботние

воскресные.

клубами расползалась паника

не отвеченных сообщений

звонков

возбужденные возгласы

уф вы живы

что там у вас происходит

по новостям сказали

что стреляют по мирным жителям

зачем только вы обратились к путину.

в сером небе ни звезд ни луны

лишь отблески взрывов

на стеклах высотки

весь мир растворился

в дыме и хаосе.

между западом и востоком

между западом и востоком

твоё да—моё нет.

аруаки

спасите меня от пустых слов

оставляющих жалкий след

да обойдет меня сеть интриг

из чужих обид.

пусть нет будет нет

без моего суда

без верхнего суда

суда потустороннего

с чувством вины
где любой шаг—
преступление за
которым следует смерть
физическая или духовная.
люди и запахи излучают:
да—каждый второй
в патологии
с явным признаком цвета кожи
нет—мир состоит
из бесцветных хамелеонов.
да обойдет меня стороной
твоё да твоё нет
родина враг сосед.

*Аруаки—(с каз. языка) духи предков.

FOG OF JANUARY

Oral Arukenova

Translated by Shelley Fairweather-Vega

I.

mama used to tell me

there's nothing more beautiful than a word

more terrible than a word

papa used to tell me

there's nothing more vital than the truth

more frightful than the truth

the she-wolf inside me whispers

there's nothing more powerful than your den

more helpless than your den

I tell myself have no fear

this is nothing but words—

the truth home blood

II. fog of january

no stars no moon in the lackluster sky

just the glint of explosions

in high-rise windows

the whole world decomposed

in chaos and smoke.

concealed in the fog

of the high and prestigious

they dripped to the center

husky and bearded

ghosts from the past:

assassins

from the lowlier places

came the angered crowds

to mount and ride

the petroleum-dollar bull

to splash their fury

on glamorous symbols

of life's own masters and civil servants.

the apple city's people
could not immediately tell
the firecrackers' bangs
from machine gun fire
from apartment windows
in hesitant trickles
through thunder and char
the prayers broke through
for morning for evening
many times over
for friday
for saturday
for sunday.
gusting the panic crept spreading
from messages unanswered
and calls
exalted exclamations
oh you're alive
what's happening where you are
they said on TV
that they're shooting civilians
why would you ever go to putin.
no stars no moon in the lackluster sky
just the glint of explosions
in high-rise windows
the whole world decomposed
in chaos and smoke.

III. between west and east

between west and east
your yes is my no.
aruaqtar*
shelter me from empty words
leaving a pitiful trace
may the web of intrigue and
foreign grievances pass me by.
let no be no
without my judgment
without higher judgment

judgment otherworldly

with a sense of guilt

where any step

is a crime that

is followed by death

physical or spiritual.

people and odors both radiate:

yes—fully half of us

are pathological

with pronounced signs of skin color

no—the world consists

of colorless chameleons.

may it pass me by

your yes and your no

motherland neighbor foe.

Aruaqtar (Kazakh) are the spirits of the ancestors.

Анаста сия Белоусова

жритель окраин

окуклилась

скопила

надышала тепло

братья и сестры мои по кокону

глаза их прояснились

руки освободились для объятий

время отпустить сандалии упархивать в балконные края

время читать стихи а не новости

слушать мысли а не ютуб

время в расплавленной карамели

янтаря

вязко и жарко

а потом "по три раза ходят на опознание: алматинцы не хотят верить в смерть"

протянулась пуповина

ледяной иглой всеклась в заворот пупка

10.01.2022, Алматы

[UNTITLED] "AN INHABITANT OF THE OUTSKIRTS"

Anastasiya Belousova

Translated by Katherine E. Young

an inhabitant of the outskirts
pupated
gathered and
breathed in warmth

my cocooning brothers and sisters
their eyes lit up
arms broke free for hugs

time to let go of sandals take flight for balcony realms
time to read poems and not the news
to follow thoughts and not YouTube
time in the melted caramel
of amber
gooey and hot

and then "they go three times to identify the body: Almaty's people don't want to believe in
      death"

umbilical cord stretched out
icy needle jabbing the belly button's whorl

January 10, 2022, Almaty

НЕ СТРЕЛЯЙ

Асел Омар

Спроси мое имя, пока я здесь.
Не плачь, мое сердце еще стучит,
Моя плоть превращается в глину.
На могиле моей вырастут маки,
Я верю.
На площади, уже видевшей кровь,
я не знаю, кто мне друг, и кто мне враг.
Я всего-то хотел справедливости.

Всего-то. Но ведь справедливости нет?
Спроси мое имя, пока жива моя мать.
Я поднял руки вверх,
Не вижу лиц тех, кто смотрит на меня в прицел.
Не вижу шевронов—
Слишком густой туман в январе,
И небо бело от вспышек гранат.
Ты же видишь, я безоружен.

Вожди называют нас великим народом
с телеэкранов,
Я стою здесь, подняв руки,
И мне все равно, как они нас назовут.
Ты просто не стреляй.
Не стреляй в меня.

Спроси мое имя, когда маки расцветут на моей могиле,
Когда тело мое станет частью земли.
Спроси мое имя, пока я здесь,
Слишком густ белый туман вокруг,
Это не автоматная очередь, не шумовая граната,
это сердце мое стучит
в последний раз.
Мама, это все еще я, прости.
Не плачь, просто сегодня слишком густой туман,
Слишком белое небо,
В которое я улетаю.

DON'T SHOOT

Asel Omar

Translated by Shelley Fairweather-Vega

Ask my name while I am here.
Don't cry. My heart is still beating,
My flesh is turning to clay.
Poppies will grow on my grave,
I have faith.
On the square, which has seen blood before,
I don't know who's a friend, who's a foe.
All I wanted was justice.

Only that. But maybe there is no justice?
Ask my name while my mother is alive.
I put my hands up,
I can't see the faces of the ones who have me in their sights.
I can't see their chevrons—
The January fog is much too thick,
And the sky's gone white from exploding grenades.
You can see, though: I'm unarmed.

The chieftains call us a great people
from the television screens,
I'm standing here, my hands up,
And I don't care what they call us.
Just please don't shoot.
Don't shoot me.

Ask my name when the poppies flower on my grave,
When my body becomes a part of the earth.
Ask my name while I am here,
The white fog is too thick around me,
That's not machine gun fire, not a stun grenade,
that's my heart beating
for the last time.
Mama, it's still me. I'm sorry.
Don't cry, it's just that the fog is too thick today,
Too white, the sky
I am flying away into.

ЭТО В МЕНЯ СТРЕЛЯЛИ

Канат Омар

когда пожилые родители пересидев у дочери все три кошмарных дня

и заставив сидеть с ними сына

который поначалу рвался на площадь чтобы видеть своими глазами

как народ наконец говорит

пусть неумело косноязычно задыхаясь от ярости но честно

и оттого речь его чиста

а потом увидев по центральному телеканалу

(потому что интернет сразу отключили а независимых журналистов

сделали зависимыми от воли случая и пули-дуры)

погромщиков с их криворотыми предводителями

тех самых титушек знакомых по зарубежным новостям прошлого десятилетия

а следом за ними трясущихся от вожделения мародёров

рушащих любимый город

то сразу как-то сник и просидел с ними вместе

все эти три дня

со стариками сестрой и племянниками

так вот когда пересидев три дня у дочери и дождавшись затишья

пожилая пара отвозит сына на стареньком митсубиши до самой его квартиры

чтобы с ним ничего по пути не случилось и затем успокоенная

возвращается наконец домой

её без предупреждения расстреливают военные

прицельным огнём на поражение

очень точным как на стрельбище или экзамене на политическую зрелость

умение стремительно развернуться по ветру

и сохранить невозмутимость

как будто бы это совсем не позорно и несгибаемые предки столетиями

учили именно этому

и автомобиль взрывается и горит на перекрёстке

как во время войны

которую объявили себе

не спросив никого

и никто его не тушит потому что никому нет дела

и сын всё никак не может дозвониться до стариков

и потом они с сестрой ищут по всему городу

звонят в полицию больницы морг

и только на четвёртый день находят останки автомобиля

на том самом перекрёстке

и сын собирает пошатываясь

рассыпающийся пепел любимых

обугленные косточки матери

хрупкий как ёлочная игрушка из новогоднего детства череп отца

и никак не может отскоблить

от металлического остова

драгоценную присохшую грязь

шепчущуюся с ним золу

и тогда ему помогают сделать то что он должен

те кто уже давно мертвы

когда об этой истории

как и многих таких же

—о застреленных детях о сгоревших заживо семьях о пулевых отверстиях в окнах мирных домов—

рассказывает жена

её рука с чашкой дрожит и красный остывший чай едва не выплёскивается на белоснежную

рубашку с короткими рукавами

а почему она в рубашке когда за окном январь

ведь она сидит за кухонным столом у окна и смотрит не отрываясь на улицу

от которой тянет холодом

кто мне ответит

5 февраля 2022

THIS IS THEM SHOOTING AT ME

Kanat Omar

Translated by Shelley Fairweather-Vega

after his elderly parents have been hunkered down at their daughter's place three nightmarish days

and they made their son sit with them, too

at first he'd been out on the square to see with his own eyes

how the people were finally speaking up

honestly even if clumsily tongue-tied and gasping with fury

which made their speech pure

but once they'd seen on the government channel

(because the internet was immediately shut down and independent journalists

were made dependent on the will of fate and stray bullets)

the marauders and their wry-mouthed ringleaders

the same titushki they all knew from the international news of this past decade

and behind them looters quivering with lust

destroying the city they loved

Then the son wilted quickly and went to stay with them

all those three days

with the old folks and his sister and nephews

so after they've sat at their daughter's place for three days until it is calmer

the elderly couple drives their son in their old Mitsubishi to his own neighborhood

to make sure nothing happens to him on the way and then feeling relieved

finally set off for home

they are shot without warning by soldiers

targeted fire shooting to kill

with great precision like target practice or a test of political maturity

the skill for quickly twisting in the wind

and maintaining impassivity

as if there were nothing shameful about it and their stalwart ancestors spent centuries

teaching them nothing but this

and the vehicle explodes and burns at the crossroads

like in a time of war

that has declared itself

without asking anyone

and nobody puts it out because it's nobody's business

and the son can't seem to get a call through to the old folks
and then he and his sister search the whole city
they call the police and hospitals and morgue
and it's only on day four they find the car's remains
right there at the crossroads

and the son is shaking as he collects
the scattered ashes of his parents
the small and blackened bones of his mother
his father's skull fragile as a pine-tree bauble from a boyhood holiday
and he just cannot scrape
the priceless baked-on grime
with the ashes stuck in it
from the metal frame
and then they help him do what he must
those who died long ago

when this story
as well as the many like it
—of executed children families burned alive bullet holes in windows of residential buildings—
is told by his wife
the teacup shakes in her hand and the cold red tea almost splashes on her snow-white
short-sleeved blouse
and why is she wearing short sleeves when it's January out there through the window
she's sitting at the kitchen table by the window after all her eyes are glued to the street
from where the cold seeps in
who can tell me

February 5, 2022

КОЛЫБЕЛЬНАЯ

Рамиль Ниязов

I.

аул уехал в даль
словно в волчью ловушку
ты залей слова мама́
в моё пустое ушко

укради меня туда где течёт
Есентай под родимый кров
а не вен фабричный
берёзовый сок

и красная сперма-краска
аткян чаем рассвета ставшая

мы пьём его ночью
и зубы крошатся

а по арыкам
то солёным то сладким
течёт ледяной
пресной кипяток

и до звезды достаёт

бирюза

на вкус что
будто святой была

II.

где Фурманова вспоротое брюхо
почему-то оказалось пусто
саркыт бедным стала пустота
богатым—садака

на весь чёрный свет поминальный плов
в белоснежном казане приготовь
от сглаза занавес алый навесь

в на солнце сгнившее мясо
что называлось бог
чистые бритвы руками грязными
положи под язычок

III.

семью звездами стакан
нефтью огранённый до дна
залей в каспийское море рта
сердце прополоскать

сигарету об грудь затуши
белый буран
попробуй вкусить

—

он почти как «берёзовый сок» —
как то самое
ненужное детство —
вкусный и ненастоящий

—

он почти что
святой
и признает ли мать
одного

из пропавших своих сыновей
по тавру
под отрубленным язычком

LULLABY

Ramil Niyazov

Translated by Katherine E. Young

I.
the *aul* moved off into the distance
as if into a wolf trap
pour the words mama
into my empty little ear

steal me away to where
the Esentai flows beneath my beloved home
and not a factory-made vein
birch juice

and red cum-paint
has become salty *atkyan,* the tea of dawn

we drink it at night
and our teeth crumble

and along the irrigation ditches
either salty or sweet
flows icy-
fresh boiling water

and turquoise

as if it
were holy to the taste

reaches for the stars

II.

where Furmanov's split belly
for some reason turned up empty
emptiness became leftovers for the poor
sadaka for the rich

cook a commemorative feast for the whole black world
in a snow-white cauldron
hang a scarlet curtain against the evil eye

in the sun-rotted meat
that was called god
lay clean razors under the tongue
with dirty hands

III.

pour a glass with seven stars
faceted to the bottom with oil
into the Caspian Sea of your mouth
to rinse your heart

put out a cigarette on your chest
a white snowstorm
try to taste it

—

it's almost like birch juice—
like that
unnecessary childhood—
delicious and unreal

—

it's almost
holy
and does a mother recognize
one

of her missing sons
by the brand
beneath his severed tongue

Ирина Гумыркина

***

И страшно так, Господи, страшно—
Уже невозможен побег:
Чернеет на площади башня,
И замертво падает снег.

За краем, за раем, за воем
Не видно, не слышно Тебя.
Нас перекроили без воли—
Узнаешь ли прежних, скорбя?

По буквам читай эсэмэски,
Молчи, как молчит «Телеграм».
Почти невозможно, но если—
Нас всех—отпусти до утра.

[UNTITLED] "AND IT'S SCARY, LORD, IT'S SCARY—"

Irina Gumyrkina

Translated by Katherine E. Young

And it's scary, Lord, it's scary—
There's no more escape to be had:
The tower showing black on the square,
And snow falling as if dead.

Beyond the edge, heaven, the howl,
I can't see You, I can't hear.
We've been remade against our will—
Will You recognize us, grieving?

Spell out every SMS,
Hush, like Telegram: go dormant.
It's near impossible, but if
You can: release us all till morning.

Ирина Гумыркина

***

Этот город увековечен
В «Шаныраке» и «Акбулаке»,
В кетлинге и кибербуллинге,
В «Сулпаке» и реновации,
В исчезнувших трамваях,
Исчезающей мозаике,
В сгоревших памятниках
Советской архитектуры.

В январском тумане
Скрывается нечто ещё—
Если найдёшь какую-то связь,
Напиши петицию
В небесную канцелярию,
Чтобы было что рассказать
Следующему поколению.

[UNTITLED] "THIS CITY'S IMMORTALIZED"

Irina Gumyrkina

Translated by Katherine E. Young

This city's immortalized
In Shanyrak's trauma, Akbulak's,
In kettling by police,
In cyberbullying,
In rebuilds, trees cut down
To "beautify" Sulpak,
In long-vanished tramlines,
In a missing mosaic,
In the burned-out landmarks
Of Soviet architecture.

Something else is hidden
In January's mist—
If you find any connection,
Offer up a petition
To the chancery of the heavens
So you'll have something to say
To the coming generation.

[UNTITLED] "THIS CITY'S IMMORTALIZED"

DEAR PLUTO

Susan L. Lin

DEAR PLUTO,

I'm writing to share my plans to visit you in the distant future. You'll be the ball of ice and rock in the Kuiper Belt. I'll be the figure wearing the spacesuit, stepping off the spacecraft, making my way through the spacegalaxy. If my calculations are correct, I'll reach you in a decade. I hope you'll be waiting at the end of my journey. We can throw a party when I finally land, print B.Y.O.R. on the invites.

B.Y.O.R. = Bring Your Own Rings

Yes, I know you don't usually accessorize. I don't either. But my arrival will be a special occasion, as good an excuse as any to raid our jewelry boxes. Maybe Saturn will watch the festivities from afar with envy. Uranus, Jupiter, and Neptune, too. That clique right there loves to flaunt their rings at every hour of every day for all the solar system to see.

I've started and restarted this letter a dozen times, unsure where to begin. I'm afraid there's no way of writing it that doesn't paint me a stalker in desperate need of a restraining order. Maybe that's exactly what I am. It's true that you don't know me. It's true that we've never met. I've never even laid eyes on you in person-planet. (I don't own a telescope, and even if I did, spying on you without your knowledge seems even more deplorable.)

But I was a toddler when I first saw your picture on glossy posters of the Milky Way that used to hang in my bedroom. The complimentary ones folded between pages of *National Geographic* magazines, to which my father was an avid subscriber. You were that dot on the outermost reaches of the solar system, rejected from a prime location in the inner circle. Even at a young age, I could imagine how isolating that must've felt.

I was seven when I began learning more about the history of you. Every time my teacher wheeled the LaserDisc player into the storage closet, I knew we'd be treated to more animations of celestial bodies that were, like all of us, orbiting the sun. Being packed into that tiny space like tinned fish didn't bother me because there you were, again, on that grainy screen: taking the scenic route through the darkness, patiently carving your own path around everyone else.

That same year, I memorized the universal mnemonic device for recounting the order of the planets.

My Very Educated Mother Just Served Us Nine Pizzas = Mercury, Venus, Earth, Mars, Jupiter, Saturn, Uranus, Neptune, Pluto

The local pizza buffet advertised a special for Wednesdays, emblazoned on their windows: all-you-can-eat pizza, pasta, and salad for the low price of $1.99, with kids under ten devouring everything in sight for only 99 cents. Whenever we dined there, I thought of you.

I was eight when my homeroom teacher measured and weighed us to begin the year. At four-feet-zero and forty-eight pounds, even after putting away all that bread and cheese, I remained the smallest in my class. Another dubious distinction we held in common. I wonder if, like me, you grew up binge-eating space junk because you hoped you could one day balloon out like Jupiter? I bet you understood the embarrassment of being the only planet in the galaxy unable to donate a piece of yourself to help others in need.

I was ten when I started writing letters. My elementary school believed in Routines. My elementary school believed in The Arts. My elementary school believed, above all else, in Acronyms. And so, our principal decreed that the first school hour of every Monday would be W.I.S.H. time.

W.I.S.H. = Writing Is Special Here!

Maybe I should've tried to contact you as early as then. I'm sorry now that I didn't. We could've been pen pals trading anecdotes back and forth for decades. I could've read your life story in your own words instead of believing the passages in a science textbook written by yet another human who'd never met you. The truth is, by that time I had forgotten about you. The truth is, something deeply traumatic happened to me the year before, when I was nine. I no longer trusted anybody, even if said body happened to be a hunk of space rock 2.66 billion miles away.

I thought, foolishly, that if I didn't think about it, it couldn't hurt me anymore.

I was eleven when I saw my former B.F.F. again. We crossed paths at the local pizza buffet, of all places. I was with my family. (She no longer had one.) She was with her new friends. (I no longer had any.) "Hi!" she exclaimed, stopping in her tracks on the way to an empty table, as if she had never chosen, repeatedly, to inflict physical harm. "Hi!" I exclaimed, a half-eaten slice between my lips, as if I had never lived in a constant state of terror every second she was near. In that moment, I wasn't thinking about what she'd done to me. I wasn't even thinking about you. I wasn't thinking about much of anything but the unfinished crunchy taco pizza on my plate.

B.F.F. = Best Friend Fornever

Crunchy Taco Pizza = crisp paper-thin crust + hot sauce + ground beef + shredded lettuce + shredded cheese

I wished I could shred all my memories from that lost year until they were unrecognizable, illegible, impossible to put back together. But that would mean losing the bright spots that shimmered like stars on the fringe of a black hole: organizing a renegade Pizza Party the month before the 1996 Presidential Election; building a miniature house with working electricity out of paperclips, brass brad fasteners, and battery packs; standing on stage in front of the whole school during R.I.F. week and reading aloud from my winning essay about the importance of literacy.

R.I.F. = Reading Is Fun . . . damental!

I was nineteen when I found out you weren't a planet anymore. Reading news of the controversial decision, on the front page of the *Houston Chronicle* a mere month after my summer Astronomy 101 course concluded, was no fun at all. A childhood refrain returned to me, unbidden, as I sat at the kitchen table you were now being denied a seat at:

My Very Educated Mother Served Us Nine—
My Very Educated Mother Served Us Nine—

Suddenly, we weren't allowed to finish the thought.

Indeed, the local pizza buffet was still thriving twelve years later. In fact, they'd recently moved to a larger plot of land that faced the state highway. An adult plate now cost upwards of $7. They didn't even offer habitual discounts anymore. We still ate there anyway, sometimes. But I no longer thought of you when we did.

I was almost twenty-five the first time I discovered someone who hadn't heard the news of your demotion, and for a brief moment, the idea of it warmed my heart. For a brief moment, I wanted to live in her oblivious world. Then she spent the rest of our lunch casting aspersions on a mutual family member and banishing a fellow human being's dreams into the ether. We went our separate ways without a word about my imminent birthday.

Another eight years would pass before I fully rediscovered my love for the cosmos, trust issues be damned.

And so I'm writing today to share my plans to visit you in the distant future. If you say no, I will respect your decision. I will not don my spacesuit, and I will not enter my spacecraft, and I will not begin making my way through our spacegalaxy.

I hope you say yes. In ten years time, I hope I'll be there—with rings on.

LIGHTING CANDLES FOR A LOCAL OSIRIS[1]

Daryl Lim Wei Jie

The Malaysian poet and writer Wong Phui Nam died on the 26th of September, 2022, in his sleep. I will always remember waking up to a text from his son, Sha'arin, informing me of this bald fact—*My father passed away at 1050pm last night.* In the haze and grog of the early morning, I wondered briefly if this was some deranged joke. I had just seen the man two days before, in his home in Brickfields, Kuala Lumpur. The pandemic had scuttled a planned trip in March 2020, then kept us apart for two long years.

He was immobile and confined to the house, but was otherwise in good spirits. He hoped to recover fully by December, so he could head to the optician's to get his reading glasses adjusted. I found him as sharp as ever, and still deeply interested in literary goings-on in Singapore and Malaysia. Two hours of conversation, punctuated with frequent laughter, passed by swiftly. Toward the end of the afternoon, he said he was still writing poems and revising them, and that he wished to publish a final book. *He waited for you*, my mum said to me afterward.

Yet his death does not come as a surprise—and though it sounds strange to say it, I do not think it surprised him. (*Personally I think I have outlived my time*, he texted me in August this year.) No other poet I know had so thoroughly prepared himself for death, contended with its shadowy mysteries. Death suffuses his work, acting as a catalyst of deeper truths about the exilic migrant condition that he perceived himself to be stranded in—and the broader human condition. That he found in ancient Egypt fertile ground to cultivate his own peculiar strain of myth is, in hindsight, entirely apt. One might even say he was fascinated by the scythe's inarguable sweep.

Even as he approached the end, he faced it squarely, writing in a very recent unpublished poem, 'Ruminations at Dawn':

> But the present filters out the senses from all else
> but from itself, making it real, and we have to endure it.
> Yet the present too is a passing dream, from which
> we will salvage nothing, not even ourselves.[2]

* * *

Death was a frequent visitor during Wong's childhood. His mother died when he was four, at the age of thirty-six, from kidney failure. His father would die during the Japanese occupation, due to complications from diabetes. His store of insulin had expired; the hospital had no antibiotics to treat the ulcer on his foot, which became infected and gangrenous. This death

---

[1] I would like to thank Tse Hao Guang and Yeow Kai Chai for reading drafts of this piece and providing their thoughtful comments.
[2] I am grateful to Brandon Liew for making available recordings of Wong Phui Nam's work, which were prepared for the exhibition 'A Wasteland of Malaysian Poetry in English', which was held from 20 August to 9 September 2022 in Kuala Lumpur. Wong recorded these poems in August 2022.

would turn up, years later, in the book *Remembering Grandma and other Rumours* (1989), with Wong imagining his father on his deathbed in the hospital:

> Out of each unquiet night
> there grows the sense that I am but remnant
> cast up from another life, nothing that is wholly
> man, thrown up log-like, upon the beach, this bed.

Remembering Grandma expresses his horror at death—not at its inevitability, but how its coming exposed the emptiness of the lives of his relatives, given over to sensuality and weaknesses of the flesh. *I looked at the lives of my relatives and saw the failure of their lives in the crisis they underwent when they sensed their impending end*, he said in an interview.

I can't help but think of his father's infected foot, though, described grotesquely by Wong as a "tight congested melon, ready to give out / its soft pulp at a touch". I can't help thinking of Wong Phui Nam's own infected foot, which prevented him from walking in his last days. Of course, he wrote about it:

> Pain ignited in the deep trench of my foot,
> where skin and flesh has been sheared,
> sheared off with some bone,
> engulfs me in a fiery, insistent present
> that is also the past.

That is also the past?

* * *

Twenty years old, Wong Phui Nam travelled from Kuala Lumpur to Singapore to begin his university education at the University of Malaya. The year was 1955. Singapore would achieve limited self-government that year, with the election of its first chief minister, David Marshall. As anticipation of eventual liberation from colonial rule grew, an incipient Malayan consciousness was coming into being.

The university had only become a full-fledged university six years prior, in 1949, a product of the merger of Raffles College and the King Edward VII College of Medicine. That year, *The New Cauldron*, a student magazine, began publication. The magazine set out lofty visions of a national literature:

> The people of Malaya are a mixed crowd. . . . A Malayan language will arise out of the contributions these
> communities will make to the linguistic melting pot. The emerging language will then have to wait for a
> literary genius who will give it a voice and a soul, a service which Dante performed for the Italian language.

In an atmosphere of febrile excitement, aspiring undergraduate writers experimented with this melding of languages, dubbed *Englmalchin*. Wang Gungwu recalls that "the last months of 1949 were an intensive period of experiment", with madcap monstrosities such as *Itu stamp ta' ada gum ta' boleh stick-lah* the result. But in the end, the writers eventually decided "to write with English as [a] base". The next year, Wang would publish his landmark attempt at a Malayan English poetry, the volume *Pulse*. Yet by 1955, *The New Cauldron* would declare Engmalchin "a failure . . . because of its self-conscious artificiality".

* * *

Enter Wong Phui Nam and his associates, Tan Han Hoe and Oliver Seet. They steered the search for a new national literature in a different direction. Inspired by the French symbolists, Wong in the *New Cauldron* urged violence against the English language in service of a Malayan poetry:

> To write poems expressing the Malayan national character . . . our future poets must indulge in, to misquote
> Rimbaud, a "reasoned derangement of" English forms of usage of the language. We can even expect violence
> in the syntax if necessary.

Wong and Tan edited *Litmus One* (1958), an anthology of thirteen poets, hoping that the book "could be a backbone for future verse-writers so that they need not work out their own system of symbols". This energy culminated in Wong's early chapbook, *Toccata on Ochre Sheaves* (1958), which attempted to build Malayan poetry on the myths and symbols of ancient Egypt. Though he later disavowed the book, his ability to evoke mounting disquiet in an alien landscape still holds power:

> Within the abacus of my thought I cannot add
> Or subtract the moon from upgashed furrows.
> Along stone corridors of the ordered hill
> The wind crept unseen, divorced of leafvoices.

Looking up my copy of his collected *An Acre of Day's Glass* (2006), I realise that these four lines, like weary refugees, have survived the years, somewhat changed, and made their home in another sequence of poems, 'First Notes'.

* * *

What Wong Phui Nam really wanted to write was music. When I interviewed him in KL in 2019, he spoke of how *frankly ecstatic* he was when he first encountered classical music as a child. *Much more so than when I came to poetry*, he quipped. He tried to write pieces for the piano, but was unable to test them on the actual instrument. After the death of his father, the main breadwinner, his family was much too poor to afford a piano or hire a teacher.

His foray into musical composition crashed devastatingly into reality when a classmate in school attempted to play his piece. *It didn't sound like it had anything to do with a piano.*

> *Then what else could I write? I started writing poetry as the next best thing.*

* * *

Yet music was ever on his mind. His chapbook was a toccata: a short, virtuosic piece intended to showcase the musician's dexterity. In his final year in university, he started writing a sequence titled 'Nocturnes and Bagatelles'. Nocturnes are musical compositions inspired by the night—Chopin was a famed exponent—and we can perhaps hear a faint forlorn strain in these lines:

> Evening settles in under a flat sky
> upon a heart stricken with its emptiness.
> You will not look upon my house, my broken garden
> with frangipani by wire-fence strung with rain.

In *How the Hills are Distant*, his first mature poems, he cast himself as an Orpheus figure, coaxing music out of hard ground:

> I may be ready for the torment which infects
> a new beginning—to be my lute's flame
> to charm these manic buildings, the columns
> and mindless walls, withholding monsters
> . . . to sue
> out of a paranoiac darkness for a forgotten eurydice.

In his final years—in Chinese, we call them "night years"—he seemed to be straining to hear another kind of music. Upon turning eighty-six, he wrote:

> . . . I am of an age
> old enough to hear silence
> in the winnowing in the wind of turning days,
> hear it in dream, from intent listening—
> . . .
> as acuteness of ear comes with age,
> silence grows ever louder.

* * *

One of Wong Phui Nam's books is titled *Against the Wilderness*. I don't think he was being melodramatic. In university, he faced down the hostility of the university's English lecturers, who deeply disapproved of his literary activities. They threatened to fail him and those who associated with him. For this reason, Wong didn't qualify for a degree in English, and only in Economics. Wong summarised these attitudes in an interview, with a characteristically wry coda:

> All English poetry was holy writ. How dare we Asiatics even think of adding to it . . . 'If you have not imbibed
> the language with your mother's milk, you will never have an ear for it, you see.' (Actually, what one imbibes
> is baby talk with one's mother's milk.)

Even as he overcame these doubts about writing in English to produce some spectacular breakthroughs in poetry, culminating in *How the Hills are Distant* in 1968, fresh crises arose due to the political situation in Malaysia.

The riots of 13 May 1969, arising from deep communal tensions, provoked two major shifts that occurred in 1971: one economic, one cultural. Famously, the New Economic Policy sought to reduce ethnic economic disparities, with an eventual target stating that the Bumiputera (indigenous people) ought to hold a 30 percent share of the equity in Malaysia. Relatively less attention has been paid to the role of the National Culture Policy, which asserted that the national culture of Malaysia had to be based on the indigenous culture of the region. English literature was relegated to a "sectional" literature.

This situation silenced Wong, for about two decades, reducing him to a "fierce . . . charred mute" (to quote a poem he wrote after Rimbaud). Reflecting upon this in 2006, he said:

> The language situation created grave doubts for me about my writing. I felt then that, by writing in English,
> perhaps I would never be able to draw on the 'authentic' life of this country. I questioned myself as to the
> legitimacy of my writing and I questioned myself into silence for quite a long while.

* * *

To encounter Wong Phui Nam's poetry for the first time is to be plunged into a dark, alien landscape of foreboding, even hostile presences. Unregenerate beasts, demons and malevolent gods range the land. It is a world that actively resists interpretation:

> You who would look for signs, or starve
> among a wilderness of stone, there are only the boulders
> drowning in pits of worked out mining leases.
> From the main street of the town,
> see how the hills are distant, locked in their silences.

Yet scholars have tried, and have read in the poems of *How the Hills are Distant* an expression of the migrant, exilic condition. Wong himself provided the clues, expressing his horror at the barren circumstances of his ancestors, who arrived in a "culturally (and spiritually) denuded state", armed only with debased religious rituals, which he deemed "scant inheritance . . . to contend with the wilderness." This deprivation he would explore in a personal way in *Remembering Grandma*.

Others read into the poems the frustration of an attempt to articulate a unified, national consciousness. Again, Wong was his own explicator, stating that

In cultural terms, the Malaysian psyche is a naked one. . . . We clothe our nakedness in tatters stripped from mutually unrelated cultures to which we severally claim to be heirs but which are not ours as a single people. I have thus come to see my work as a progressive mapping of this unprotected state.

One way of seeing it is that his poetry represents an aborted Malayan culture, an undead abomination staggering across the peninsula, searching for a home.

This seems to be a country where I have lost my way . . .

* * *

Increasingly, I have come to think of his poetry as a type of world-building. I take seriously his pronouncement that he has written *for those who truly understand what it means to have to make one's language as one goes along.* Every nerd knows you only create a language so you can build a world around it.

I think this Wong-world, despite its sometimes perverse bleakness, was a means by which he understood the perplexing conditions and contradictions that engulfed him. A country that sidelined him and the language he wrote in (. . . yet he married a Malay woman, and converted to Islam). Separation from his closest compatriots: Oliver Seet and Tan Han Hoe suddenly became Singaporeans, after Singapore separated from Malaysia on 9 August 1965. The departure of other promising English poets from Malaysia, like Ee Tiang Hong and Shirley Lim. His own work in merchant banking, which must have rubbed up against his own persistent sense of living in a wilderness "serving the imperatives of commodity markets", as he said in his introduction to *Against the Wilderness* (2000).

The world he constructed he had control of. He could be its main maker of meaning, or lack thereof. It was a realm of the "sick consciousness", the wounded psyche. In this realm he battled himself and the demons that arose, decade after decade.

In a review of his collected work in 2007, Shirley Lim would comment: "It is when Wong forgets his losses . . . that his achievement as Anglophone poet of Malaysia's polyglot peoples and histories is most persuasive."

Yet what is Wong Phui Nam without his losses?

* * *

His poetry is like some varieties of Chinese tea, I remarked to a friend. After one has gotten through the bitterness, there is an exquisite sweetness. *This describes a shuixian I just had over the weekend,* was the reply.

There are redemptive moments of lightness in his poetry, which feel like hard-won victories. In 'Temple Caves', we are in another part of the Wong-world. (He told me its images were inspired by the Batu Caves, a significant Hindu holy site just outside Kuala Lumpur.) We journey through these not-Batu caves and descend into a harrowing realm of superstition and blindness not unlike Plato's allegorical darkness. The statues of the gods here are *mere torsos, stiffened rib cages locked with wire / and heads hardened about bent pig-iron rod.* We are asked, rhetorically, *What can they suggest?* The answer:

> All that we can hope to know about being more
>
> than merely human is held fast, mixed in with coarse grain
>
> in bodies, calcified into substance
>
> that daily becomes more solid, more resistant than stone.

As we descend, the darkness deepens, *it thrusts itself into the face and teeth . . . it beats back upon us our dis-ease.* We are trapped in *a dream of fury that would not subside.*

Yet in the last section of the sequence we are told that *it has been rumoured there are exits / in the most unexpected places.* The poem ends on a prophecy. The sun, once caught in a massed entanglement of coiled roots, will tear and free itself:

> Breaking out of the earth it will ascend
>
> taking to itself half of the heavens, reveal itself
>
> a tremendous bird of lightning, of the source of light,
>
> bird that cleaves the world to itself in a consuming fire.

* * *

'Temple Caves' first appears in *Remembering Grandma,* and I find it interesting that the images of this prophecy are so precisely a reversal of the ending of a poem in the same book dedicated to his brother, who died of cancer:

> Out of the melting heat of fierce corruption
>
> there rose no other, no spreading of great wings,
>
> no bird of renewal, bird out of the cleansing fire.

Though Wong was horrified by his clan's futile struggles against death, he seems to have believed there was some possibility of spiritual truth that could emerge from properly reckoning with death.

In 'Imago', the last poem of *Remembering Grandma,* this truth, addressed directly as a *you,* is described as a grub-like potentiality residing in each person. *You are faint imprint, of life / still to be received.* It bides its time to one day be *the revealed imago, perfect / in limb, in wing.* This fully formed creature will *rise, in due time, soar beyond / the common dust of day.* Yet the speaker still declares himself *too much of the flesh.* We leave him, awaiting this epiphany, *in uncertainty of the hour.*

* * *

It is this same universal reality or truth that is being addressed in Wong's last book, *The Hidden Papyrus of Hen-taui* (2012; revised edition, 2019), which opens:

> Because we are mistaken about ourselves
> We mistake a fearsome, punishing god for you.

These poems, set entirely in ancient Egypt, ostensibly tell the story of a neophyte Egyptian priestess and her increasingly heretical thoughts. In reality, I think they tell of his own spiritual convictions. Most of us, he thinks, are lost in this present world of dreams:

> I am lost so deep in the common dream of the world,
> I cannot wake. In dreaming the world, I weave
> my own snare, a shimmering web sticky with the reality of
> a seeming world. I am as a fly enmeshed . . .

When at last, in the final poem, Hen-taui liberates herself from this deceiving dream, she says she "will wait, till cleansed / of self, for the return to being, to you, the still centre".

I return to that poem that Wong wrote upon turning eighty-six. As he journeyed to death, he stated his beliefs—and hopes—plainly, without the cloak of metaphor:

> At eighty-six I hear—yet barely
> of *sure and certain hope*
> that with the shutting down of the senses,
> the snuffing out of thought and the turning up
> of its deep roots—that after earth or after fire,
> silence at journey's end is not an utter, unremitting nothingness
> but a homecoming, a return to stillness,
> stillness that is the origin of all creatures great and small.

For a man so invested in myth and symbol, this plainness seems almost too vulnerable and naked. Like Shem and Japheth, I want to look away.

* * *

The day after I met him for the last time, I went to Kinokuniya in KLCC, easily the most prominent bookstore in all Malaysia. I stopped by the poetry section, which was amply stocked with authors from all over the world—except, I realised after a thorough, dispiriting search, Wong Phui Nam.

This then is a country where one cannot wish to be . . . where all conclusions, all arguments are broken down to miles of striations, the soft mud-flats.

* * *

My favourite sequence of his is 'Candles for a Local Osiris', from *Remembering Grandma*. Wong imagines what happens to an Osiris figure who is transplanted to a Malayan landscape. This Osiris's regenerative mission ultimately fails:

> . . . A god, that day you stalked
> your quarry till a sudden clearing in the woods
> happened on you and its changes of climate
> coursed through your veins. The flowers
> you found here were furry and green
> and could not bloom. In the undergrowth, the thing
> you surprised had the look you did not understand.
> And when remembrance of what you had done,
> or left undone, could no longer hurt you
> like a wound, under the leafy shadows
> you were made ready for death.

In these poems, Wong achieves an elemental horror that reaches heights of myth unmatched and unprecedented in poetry from this part of the world. *The stranger whose face is leprous under the road lamp / and his face clogged with new earth*. I turn his haunting phrases over in mind, and they seem as fresh as when they were written, and when I first read them seven years ago in a bookshop in Singapore.

He probably believed that his own quest to rejuvenate the land had failed. Eurydice had slipped out of his arms. Provocatively, he declared, in 2009, that Malaysian writing in English was dead.

In 1993, in an essay titled 'Out of the Stony Rubbish: A Personal Perspective on the Writing of Verse in English in Malaysia', he claimed that Malaysian writers in English were writing *largely to the dead, in Baudelaire's sense of the unborn*. He grimly hoped that *what is written will be read some time into the future*.

I am not sure about that future, and its distance from now.

* * *

In one version of the Osiris myth, Osiris is murdered by his brother Seth and dismembered, the pieces of his body scattered throughout the Nile. The body pieces are transformed to river reeds, and through this myth, the ancient Egyptians experienced the river and its legendary fertility as an emanation of a god.

I think about the very first poem of *How the Hills are Distant*, first published in *Bunga Emas* in 1964, a year after Malaysia was formed:

The old man grows,
lives from subconscious hills,
sentient in fishes and reeds that slant
towards eloquence of words.
The waterfowl cry
his flowering of vowels on the wind.

BEAUTY AND THE JINN

Rahad Abir

CW: Child rape and marriage

They say the girl is jinxed. Her mother died the day she was born. Six years later when her brother died of a snakebite, the father put the blame on her. Why didn't you die in his stead? he said. Girls are meant to end up in their husbands' houses. Who will look after me when I get old?

The girl has no friends. Women are wary of letting their children play with her. They always wonder how this poor girl called Beauty got such fair skin.

* * *

Beauty comes to the mosque with the other children for her morning Quran lesson. Some days I cannot stop looking at her. With big eyes and lush eyelashes, she has the face of a *memsahib*. Her hair is long and crow black. One day after the Arabic lesson, I tell Beauty to stay. You sweep the yard, I say, then go home.

Girls and boys leave the booklets and bookrests on the shelves before rushing out. They have been at the mosque since a little after the dawn prayers. Now, after an hour of reading at the top of their lungs, they are hungry and ready to run homeward.

Beauty waits. She sees everyone scurry away. One of the girls looks back at her, giggles, and makes off.

Beauty goes off to sweep. Pearl white prayer beads in my hand, I sit inside by the door and watch her measured movements. Halfway through her job, I call to her. Beauty drops the broom, slowly walks in, and stands before me.

How old are you? I ask.

Eleven, she says.

Sit down. I stroke my beard to gather my words.

Beauty hesitates, but does as told.

Remember my words? If I'm pleased with you, Allah will be pleased.

She nods.

You must do whatever I say. Keep in mind that my prayers can open the gates of heaven for you. But if I'm angry, I curse you, and you go straight to Jahannam.

I get up and shut the door. Eyes narrowed, Beauty gazes at me. I kneel down beside her and draw her to me. She wriggles like an earthworm trying to free herself from my tightening clasp.

This stays between you and me, I whisper in her ear. Don't tell it to anybody. Otherwise I'll curse your father, and he will die.

Let me go, Beauty flinches. Her voice quavers. Her face is bleached with fear.

* * *

I clean up the mess between her legs and help her to her feet. She is in tears, shaking slightly.

Don't cry, I say. You are fine. I remind her of my warning. My curse can kill her father. What will happen to her then? Her stepmother will kick her out of the house. She will end up begging on the street. Does she want that?

Beauty sniffles. I know she won't open her mouth. The girl won't risk losing her father when her stepmother treats her no better than a maid.

I unlatch the door. With short, slow steps, she shambles off the mosque veranda, then trudges across the yard, waddling like the ducks nearby. Her little figure disappears inch by inch behind the rain tree.

I bite my lip and sigh. Sitting down, I pull my beard bitterly. A blood spot on the *hogla* mat catches my eye.

* * *

Beauty has been absent from the morning Arabic lessons. I ask one of her neighbor girls. Beauty's sick, says the girl.

One evening, right before the *Isha* prayers, Beauty's father enters the mosque. My heart hits my rib cage hard. A tremor seizes me the whole time I lead the prayer. When the worshipers leave, Beauty's father approaches me.

Imam *shaheb*, he says, I have a small problem.

I hold my breath.

Beauty. Something is wrong with her.

W-what? I stammer.

She won't go to school, won't come to you for the Quran lesson. She's gone very quiet and timid.

Aha, I say in relief.

He scratches and lowers his head. He says that Beauty has been whining about abdominal ache and that her mother found out she has gotten her period. He pauses. And there's another issue, he says. Beauty wakes up screaming in the middle of the night.

I stroke my beard for a minute. It seems, I say, she's been caught by a dark wind. She must have gone under the banyan tree at a bad hour.

Oh no! cries the father.

Don't worry, I reassure him. Come tomorrow morning with a clean bottle of water.

* * *

The following morning Beauty's father returns.

I murmur some *duas* and *suras* to myself and blow into the bottle. Have her drink the water twice daily, I instruct him. In the morning on an empty stomach, and at night before going to bed. Within seven days she'll be normal, inshallah.

The father pays me a small fee, salaams, and leaves.

* * *

He visits me a week later. She hasn't improved at all, he tells me. She doesn't play. Doesn't speak. Besides, she seems to be afraid of men.

Hmm, I say, stroking my beard. I will make a special *tabiz* for her. Give me a couple of days.

* * *

Nothing's changed with the amulet, Beauty's father complains.

I need to see her in person, I say.

It is afternoon when I arrive at his house. I am seated in the veranda and hear yelling emanating from the back room. No, I won't go, Beauty howls.

The father drags her in front of me. The girl has grown thinner since I saw her last. Her head is hanging, dark hair blocking her profile.

Remove her hair from her face, I bid the father. The father complies.

Tell me what's bothering you, I say to the girl. Beauty, look at me. Lift your head.

The father straightens her head. But Beauty keeps her eyes fixed on the dirt floor.

Look at me, Beauty, I say louder. Can you hear me?

Beauty flings a stabbing glance at me, and, without warning, spits.

The father starts slapping her. The saliva feels hot against my face, burning my cheeks. I mop it with a kerchief.

Stop beating her, I blurt.

The father stops. Imam *shaheb*, *maaf* please, he keeps repeating. He asks me to forgive him and his unruly daughter.

Beauty is possessed, I announce.

Possessed? mutters the father. He turns pale.

Yes, a bad jinn. I pause. These evil spirits like pretty girls with long hair.

Ay hai, he breathes. What will happen now?

There is treatment. I will come tomorrow.

Before I am back at the mosque for the evening prayers, the entire village is abuzz with Beauty's possession. They say that Beauty is bewitched by a gigantic wayward jinn. They whisper that she drenched me in demonic spit.

* * *

I sit on the chair in the yard in front of Beauty's house. Men and women and scores of children are scattered around, waiting to watch me get rid of a jinn. Beauty is brought before me. Her hair is tied in a bun. I take a long moment to finger my beard. Then humming *suras* from the Quran, from time to time, I blow my breath on her, softly clap my hands and release them toward her.

Go, go, go now! I shout. Go this minute! You devil, go this minute! I walk around her blowing my breath. Last warning, devil! I roar, leave her now! Go back where you came from!

I sit back and ask Beauty's father to get me a coconut broom. He fetches one. I tap it on her right and left arms. She stares at me, eyes taut and bloodshot.

Go, go, go, I yell. Go away, right now! The broom bashes against her back, arms, and legs. You devil, tell me where you come from? Why did you take her?

Beauty's eyes are fixed on me.

Look down, I cry. Look down. But she glowers instead. I detect a demon in her eyes. The broom in my hand goes wild, whacking her nonstop. She convulses with every blow.

Take her, I command the father. Dip her in the water ten times.

He pulls her to the pond. I stand at the edge and count the dipping.

The father gets out of the water lugging her sopping body in his arms. Beauty is panting and shivering.

That's all for today, I say. We start again tomorrow.

* * *

The next day I chop off her hair to her chin. As her tresses fall rippling in a heap around her, I catch a collective *oh dear!* resonating among the women onlookers there. Beauty makes no sound. Her glare at me is fiercer than ever. I sprinkle holy water on her face. Her eyelids do not drop.

I smack her arms with a fresh broom. She whimpers, shaking all over. Tears drip down her cheeks, her ivory arms flashing with red streaks. I order the father to dip her twenty times. When he climbs up carrying her, Beauty looks awfully small— limbs dangling from her trunk. Her teeth chatter.

I inform the father that the girl is taken over by the worst jinn I have ever seen. This jinn can just set his eyes upon anyone and possess that person. That is the reason, I explain, that Beauty stares all the time.

I instruct him to keep her separate in a room and give her only one meal a day. I hand out amulets for everyone in his house.

The father thanks me to his best ability. For my continued service, he places a five-hundred-taka bill in my palm.

* * *

Panic plagues the villagers. Stories go around that Beauty frequently bursts out laughing and crying. They can even hear her from their houses. I hear that they walk away upon seeing Beauty's father on the street. They have stopped visiting his house and keep a strict watch on their children so no one can go near that jinn-possessed den.

I make *tabiz* amulets all day. Villagers pay me in advance and wait for hours outside the mosque to get their holy lockets stuffed with Quranic verses. Everyone wants a safeguard against the silent staring demon.

* * *

After the dawn prayer, some village elders sit with me at the mosque. They ask me to find a solution for Beauty. The ostracism of her family has to end. The girl's family is suffering, they say. They hesitate for a while, then suggest that I marry the girl. The father is happy to offer me a moderate dowry.

For a moment I cannot speak, I think of her death glare. A possessed girl, I say, shaking my head.

You can cure the girl, they say. She will be okay. She is a good girl, you know.

Yes, I know. But she's still a child.

She is almost twelve—a marriageable age. And—they add in a hushed tone, she has bled. She is a woman now.

I do not respond.

They whisper to each other. They hold my hands and plead with me, saying that this is the only way to resolve this.

We don't see any problem with it, they say. You're young too.

I keep silent. They say Beauty's stepmother is pregnant; she is expecting a boy. By no means can she allow a jinn-possessed girl to live in the same house.

They assert that Beauty will at least be useful in doing my household work. She can cook, clean, and wash my clothes.

I give my consent.

They fix next Friday for the wedding.

* * *

That night, I toss and turn in bed, thinking about the coming wedding. I remember the day with Beauty at the mosque. I let out a sigh looking back on the afternoon I cut her beautiful hair. I imagine her long hair falling off in a heap around her. I try to sleep, but in the dark I see Beauty staring at me. I get up and light the hurricane lamp. Yet the flame of the lamp seems glaring at me.

The story "Beauty and the Jinn" appears in *Our Many Longings: Contemporary Short Fiction From Bangladesh* (India: Dhauli Books, 2021), edited by Sohana Manzoor. Published by author's permission.

"WOE IS ME" AND "ME. ALONE."

Nima Youshij

Translated by Khashayar "Kess" Mohammadi

Translator's Note

To Iranians, free verse and contemporary poetry are synonymous with the name Nima Youshij since in Farsi the very term coined for free verse was Nima verse in honor of his colossal feat of standing against century upon century of ghazals, mathnavis, and several other forms of Persian poetry in order to create a contemporary poetry with his background in French poetics. Though Nima Youshij is perhaps the greatest contemporary figure in Persian poetry, not much of his work is translated, and not much is translated well. I have approached translating his incredibly dense and culturally complex poetry mostly through a semi-agglutinative linguistic approach similar to certain translations of Paul Celan, whose poetry was pivotal to me in unlocking the translation of Nima Youshij.

WOE IS ME

my farmland dried out
and the constant barrage
of the contrived . . .
       useless
     fruitless
   the slender crevice of my house
   pierced by the enemy's cunning gaze
      woe is me!
   prepared for the heart's sake:
   arrows poisoned by a grudge

   upon blood-smeared roads then/
   beheaded corpses
      dusted
   with ancestry-plated graves
   removes from my walls
   and places upon the soil
and from the hurt of the sorrowful

sits upon the heads plucked
narrates the story of sorrow.

woe is me!
in a night as dark as this
who shall trample
—unknowingly—
upon these heads
still shifting?
when shall silence break in this heavy night
from heads whose move and shake
weaves with enchantment each moment?
when shall a star
—liberated from the earth's corruption—
lend light to this dark-hearted night!

Passersby!
O Passersby!
tread my path. without thought my enemy arrives
slams me against the door, asks me names and addresses
woe is me!

upon which corner of this night shall I hang my ragged clothes?
so I can remove poisonous arrows from this sorrowful heart, bloodied?
woe is me!

ME. ALONE.

                    amidst pine trees
a sparse fringe atop the mountain range ahead
my figure divorced from me   how silver-sown
and I   the vagabond of this dark night
      his eyes   watchful in tears
                  from afar

      mounted on a giant's hair
but perhaps I have found a way
as I hand-walk along this darkness

  a sinkhole   a candle
and as if sharpened rock
I fall in the maw of the giant
  and under its teeth:
  sit in exhaustion
      no path ahead
      just me
sat at the pathway
in this dark night

the Peganum branches quake
  and the wind dragon-like
          slithering
    meets in this darkness
the beclouded facade of an island
  secluded at the warm heart
        of the nearby village

oblivious to all
villagers sleep
something diminishes
amidst all the diminished

Hey People!
who has heard of him?

was it perhaps that an unknown rider passed
whose white steed galloped atop the stony creek
     fed by the village's water source?

in Willow-dale he unmounted for a drink
glanced at me, and his smile blossomed
and in that moment we spoke
    though—moonrider he—
spoke no more

that lone ranger came and passed
    lost
     did he seek the Hamun lake?
or the mountain range perhaps
far from the plains
Hey! who has heard of him
  even as much as a sliver
      of news

and no one shall reply thus now
no one speaks my language

wind slithers still
and the Peganum quakes

    I tread this long path still
upon the pitch black darkness of this night still
     Me.   Alone.

MI HERMANA, EL TIERRA

Sigrid Marianne Gayangos

Haaay, mira, I really have nothing to gain from faking this, okay? Imagine all the work it would take, and for what? Para ginda mio cara na di inyo newspaper? I have done that and more in my younger years. 1964 La Hermosa Festival Miss Zamboanga, look it up. From tabloids to broadsheets, they had pictures of me in my beautiful mascota! See, I'm getting old. My sister's story did not die with her; but when I do, it will with me. Telling it to you now, and of course you decide for yourself whether you believe it or not, then perhaps, her story will yet live another life. I know, I know, you're doing your best not to snicker and you're just indulging this fool of a vieja. But, allow me to show you the room at least—

Mio hermana, you remember, was a journalist like yourself. But when she wasn't busy writing news stories, she was busy capturing stories in a different form: pictures. Go ahead, browse through those albums—I have more stacked in the office room—but these, these were some of her best shots. She was wild, passionate and willful and you can see how she willed herself into the subjects she captured here in these glossy, colorful spreads of magazines and these leaflets for various NGOs. I remember browsing through the raw shots on her computer when we were younger, the dense canopy of the oldest wani tree in Tumaga, the cascading water against the mossy tiered wall of rocks of Merloquet, wildflowers in full bloom up in the forest of Abong-Abong. Ah, mira aqui, the animals were her favorite, here a close-up of a bent-toed gecko clinging precariously to a plant stem, the elusive red-eyed black galansiyang. She would lean down over my shoulder and talk me through the whole experience of taking the photos, explaining how she would carefully crouch or patiently wait it out just to capture the perfect shot.

Then she would disappear for months, armed with just a rucksack containing her basic necessities and camera. And after each trip, when she returned home to us in downtown pueblo, she seemed less and less comfortable among us. Back then we lived in a tiny apartment on Pilar Street; this little bungalow I now stay in was rented out to a starting family. Buen familia, OFW el tata. She snapped at me one time, when I brought home a Beatles vinyl record I had borrowed from a friend, and delivered an impassioned speech on how pop-culture was the global capitalist's tool. I was only fourteen and didn't really understand what she was going on and on about. . . . I just wanted to listen to the Beatles. It was for this reason, among many others, that my sister and I grew apart and lost touch. When our mother died, followed shortly by our father, it was as though the feeble thread that linked us together had finally snapped. That is, until her letter reached my doorsteps in Dumaguete.

I had just moved to the city then, traveling from one seaside area to another, taking on odd jobs. I don't mean to brag, but with a face like mine, I was able to land quite a number of modeling jobs with little to no effort. Maskin onde yo ta anda, pirmi tiene trabaho para con migo. Later on I learned that she had been sending my college dormitory letters with attached clippings of her wildlife photography years after I had already graduated from the university. Perhaps in her mind, I had always been that cosmopolitan college girl who was forever trapped in that cozy university life. The dormitory manager, I suppose after having had enough of her flood of mail, found a way to connect the two of us and even forwarded all the unopened letters she had sent. In her latest letter, she wrote that she had just returned from a trip to one of the remote islands down south. She didn't specify if it was Tawi-Tawi or Sulu, but she said that she seemed to have caught a rather strange affliction.

She thought it was silly, but she was only following the doctor's order to find someone to help care for her until this mysterious affliction passed. She said that there were days when she was just awake for four hours, so she was messing up on the medication schedule a lot. She said, would I be kind enough to help her out just until she got better? Señor, el di mio corazon! I left Dumaguete that night, and boarded a ferry to Zamboanga.

Surprisingly, my sister was up on her feet the moment she heard me knock on the gate. Back in our childhood home, she greeted me with air-kisses on both cheeks, and I remember thinking how she smelled like loam and rain. Her dark black hair was thinning out, but it cascaded past her waist, and she wore nothing but a malong asymmetrically tied around her shoulder. I fit into her life with ease, into this barely furnished bungalow that somehow suddenly felt too small. She ushered me to our parents' bedroom, which she had now converted into a darkroom. She smiled tentatively and admitted that this was where she spent most of her waking hours, hunched over trays and bathed in red light. Film developers, stop bath, fixer. Todo aqui, she lined rows and rows of unreleased photos from all her past trips, clothespinned onto whatever objects would hold them.

Her illness had this way of enforcing intimacy between us, so for several weeks we were like two creatures carefully orbiting each other, mentally calculating just how much distance we could cover to get as close to one another. The years of estrangement were there, but she brushed off our differences as though nothing but fruit flies—bothersome things but, really, little nothings. Si nohay tu hermana, gendeh tu entiende. On rare occasions when she had enough energy to walk, we would venture out as far as Pasonanca Park, where she could inhale greedy lungfuls of fresh mountain air. Sabe tu, kame el primero plantitas. Sometimes, we would pick beautiful wild flowers that caught her fancy and transplant them back home. When the succeeding hospital appointments continued to prove futile, she asked me to bring more potted flowers and plants at home, she needed the outdoors indoors, she told me.

She asked for more fresh cuttings the remaining weeks: climbing pandan, brilliant red begonia, violet and yellow orchids, orange bougainvillea, and young ferns with fiddleheads—an array of wildflowers in loud colors against broad green leaves. Once, she told me how Zamboanga derived its name from the Malay word jambangan, which meant a place of flowers. Then she would ask me to get her a humidifier and sunlamps on timer, so her little jambangan inside our home could flourish. De locuras, I see you thinking, but these were the only things she wanted to do. By then she had given up all medical treatments . . . and bathing. Let me tell you—the musky scent that emanated inside was not entirely due to that little jungle of hers alone! She would recoil at any suggestion to rest or wash herself up, and those were really ugly moments I'd rather not revisit.

It was around the time her hair fell out that she requested more soil. Sacks and sacks of loam soil. The few hours when she remained conscious, she tiptoed about her jungle darkroom, strands of hair falling everywhere as though an animal was shedding fur. The first five sacks I had bought, she scattered around the floor. Then, I kid you not, a layer of organic compost. The topmost layer was a mixture of loamy and silty soil. She was hardly awake the next few days, and in the rare moments when she was, she would just lie on her cushion of earth and browse through the photographs she had taken. We sat together in the dark, in total silence save for the constant humming of the humidifier, and just smelled the deep rainforest scent of the room. On her last night, she asked me to put more soil over there, right where the bougainvillea made an arc, where she decided would be her final bed. She had asked me to cover her body with soil—numa mira ansina comigo—except for her face. I obliged, of course. A serene smile was plastered across her face and I watched her breath go heavy and slow until she was breathing no more.

I fell asleep there in the dirt, beside my sister. I remember expecting a lone magical flower to sprout where my sister had passed, and of course I would name the flower after her. But there was none. This isn't a fairy tale, after all. I grope for my sister's remains, but there was none either. I scrambled for the windows, the door, anything to get me out of this utter darkness. A striking dart of light, true daylight, pierced through the room. It fell across the rain-forest darkroom, splashing the wild bloom of flowers with a blinding yellow glow.

And so here I am, as you find me today, un loca vieja with her assortment of flowers and plants. My neighbors are kind and regularly check up on me, but I know that behind my back they talk about me in hushed, pitiful tones. I don't really mind. My sister, she told me, that it was the rich profusion of flowers that made the first navigators settle in old Zamboanga. I fancy myself some sort of a navigator, and I understand very well their reason for choosing to stay. Have you ever woken up to the sheer magnificence of a birdsong? Or spend the day simply mesmerized by the way the pinkish-purple vines refuse to follow any pattern? Outside the city pulsates with fast-paced life; in here, I am cocooned in this rainforest room. Soon, I know, I too shall take my rest. And I would leave as my sister did, con este tierra, where it smells faintly of my sister's hair and the sweet tang of freshly turned soil.

TUNGGU DULU

ila

(i)

When I caught sight of you under the tree, I felt my body quiver. I was astounded by the way the sun was glowing a fleshy pink: the glint of rays danced on your body almost as alive as the sea behind me. The shadows you cast, mirroring the setting sun. I could feel you spill out from where you were, right into where I was standing, like waves catching onto the shore.

At that moment, I could feel a story forming in the pit of my belly, tender and bloating from secrets that were not mine to tell. Maybe not yet.

"Tunggu. Tunggu dulu."

I could not walk any further. The tide had started to come up. I caught sight of a BTO being built, a slab of concrete with gaping little holes that seemed to scream, puncturing the horizon. Every half an hour, three giant sand piles on a small ship moved across the waters. I did not know where they came from or where they were going. Over here in this city, there were a lot of things that I did not know. I imagined little islands being born from the mouth of a ship as the sand was spilled into the sea. New islands with no names that would bear the weight of concrete public housing for our growing population.

I realised you must have witnessed it all as you sit perched under this tree. How many piles of sand had passed by today? How many in a year? Were you here when all the stilt houses were being pulled apart like limbs? Did you lose your home too?

"Tunggu."

From that day, I kept coming back to the same place, possessed by an impatience to find an ending to some story that was not mine. Possessed by your silence. I wanted to release what was growing inside me and stop the quivering that came from not knowing. I kept coming back to find you at the same spot but you were gone.

Although you never really left me.

(ii)

Are you a photographer? Wow, two cameras. Do you want to take photos of those big ships?

No, cik. I'm looking for something else. What are you doing here, cik?

Fishing, what else?

Do you fish here often?

No, I usually go to Changi. But today, I ended up here.

Cik, do you fish a lot?

I haven't gone in two years. What about you? What are you doing?

I'm doing a project, cik. I'm looking for . . .

Over his shoulder, a makeshift rack caught my eye. It was a common sight to see idols scattered around the outskirts of the beach. Sometimes placed under the trees or on the rocks. This rack however had about twenty idols, Ganeshas of different sizes and shapes. They were all placed together with such care on the precariously slanted rack. Some had barnacles growing on them. All of them were intact.

Ah, is that what you are looking for? Don't tegur and please mintak izin.

I already did, cik, dalam hati.

Good. Good.

I climbed over two or three big rocks to take a closer look. At the start of the rack made of broken pieces of wood balanced on tree trunks were two goddesses I did not recognise. From the corner of my eye, the uncle was watching me almost protectively.

Cik, you know who actually keeps these idols here?

Oh, it's the cleaner. You saw him earlier passing us on his bicycle. You know, maybe for them it's not good to throw away idols, even if they are from different religions. Even for us. If we see, we don't touch and disturb, right? Not because we believe in the same things, but we just don't.

Yes, cik. Cik, what is your name?

You can call me Cik Man.

Do you stay around here?

No, I stay quite far from here, all the way in Marsiling. Last time, when I was a boy, I used to stay in Pulau Belakang Mati.

You mean Sentosa?

Yes. I stayed at the end of the beach, next to a Japanese cemetery. When I stepped out of my house it was already the sea. Now I stay in a flat. I love fishing, you know? In my head, it becomes quiet and all I see is this.

So now when you go visit Sentosa, can you remember where exactly your kampong was?

Cik Man laughed quite suddenly, and I was laughing along as well. It was such a silly question to ask when I already knew the answer.

I hate Sentosa. So much has changed there. I cannot even recognise anything anymore. It looks like nothing is real. Like it's a khayalan. Last time we would just jump into the water from our koleks. Do you know what that is? It's like a boat. And we don't fish with this or bait.

Cik Man pointed to the one rod he had perched in the sand. A small plastic bag filled with raw prawns dangled from a tree branch. The prawns were being slowly devoured by ants.

How then did you fish, cik?

We used nets instead, hanging down from the koleks into the sea. Have you tasted fresh fish? No, not even the kinds from wet market, fresher than that. Straight from the water and into the kuali. It's so fresh you do not need to cook it with so much spices, you know. Last time I used to have my own boat, you know? But then suddenly need to pay rent, for parking, so I had to sell it away. No choice. Nothing is yours for very long.

Cik Man's eyes were gleaming as bright as the afternoon sun. The excitement in his voice was that of the same little boy that had lived by the sea many years ago. His memories prickled my skin like the salty air and felt so fresh that I was savouring every little bit of it with him.

Actually, nowadays, even the fresh fish do not taste as good as before. The sea . . . there's a lot of activities. Look at all those big ships, the factories all around the coast at Pasir Gudang. During my time the sea was thriving, alive and breathing. Laut macam dah nak nazak. Do you understand?

(iii)

"He said he was by the water and the spirit just asked him." X shared casually as she lay half-inclined on the floor. It was my first time meeting her in person, outside of a performance setting. Naturally I felt a comfort borne from a familiarity of sensing the world differently from others. I believe people like X, myself and the rare few whom I've encountered, perceive and experience realities beyond the normative five senses.

The first time I encountered X, I watched her move slowly under a harsh red light, possessed by whispers no one else could hear. X told me about how her father was leading a double life. It was only about six to seven years ago that her family found out about his other life as a medium, and what X described as his chosen family. She told me how her sister and mother had found these rituals sacrilegious and ungodly.

Several times on her Instagram posts, I kept seeing the primal and fluid movements from that first night X and I had crossed paths, different beings submerged in water. Was it the same water where her father merged with this spirit? X and I had a few conversations before we actually met that night.

 Conversation taken from Instagram chat on 11th of October, 2020:

Do you go into trance yourself? I'm always so fascinated when it's passed down through lineage.

My performance work definitely has some of that DNA but I don't actually go into trance. Even though I think the overlap is uncanny. Though some people said I do, but I'm not confident in calling claim to it haha

My paternal side is a family of healers so I get that sensing and on my maternal side I get the gift of telek or clairvoyance. Like knowing that something bad is going to happen but having no way to stop it? So sometimes it can be quite a curse, omg.

Ah, that's so fascinating, thanks for sharing. Yeah I can imagine. I think it requires a lot of conscious boundary setting because you can catch a lot of unwanted energies.

Sometimes when people tell me their personal experiences or their dreams, I can see it so clearly and distinctively and it can be so exhausting.

I can imagine! It's beyond empathy. It's literally inhabiting the experience. Can be quite intense. My father has always been spiritual. When I was a kid, he disappeared to Thailand for a couple of months without notice and was like a monk there for a while.

So fascinating, thanks for sharing!

Haha, np. I'm proud of my dad haha I think what he's doing is a huge part of culture here. Something that hasn't been co-opted by the government or sanitised to become more palatable for like a western audience.

Yeah or destroyed by capitalism.

Hahah, yeah once in a while you get some clueless student wandering around . . .

I mean documentation makes it visible yes but it's also how the research is framed. I'm trying to find out different rituals done at sea, not only the ones practiced by the Malays.

Yeah I think it's diminished to like folk ritual or heritage when it's so much richer than that.

Yes precisely. So hard to explain this sometimes.

Like I hate that most 'civilized' people see themselves apart from this.

That this is beyond the 'festival'

Yeah, it's a life practice as well and it permeates every aspect of lived experience and also how we perceived things. That's why I feel that people who don't engage with this, even in just simply acknowledging it are killing part of themselves.

I think it takes time to understand it beyond what is obvious. Or sometimes it doesn't happen for the person and that's ok too. It not meant for them.

Yeah sometimes it's easier to just turn a blind eye also. It's easier to live in the world and just concern yourself with material things.

Haha.

I think the developing infrastructure here also gives the illusion that this doesn't exist anymore. When really the foundations of Singapore are so occult.

*

I caught a glimpse of the fleshy pink and felt that quiver, a low rumbling in my belly as if you were turning inside me whispering your secrets in a language I could not translate. I wanted to tell X how the city woke up at odd hours of the night, fiercely alive with energies that I could never articulate and how I seemed to know which places to avoid by the way my skin folded into itself and my bones jolted in surprise. I wanted to tell X that the sensing was incomplete, unfinished and that I was an illiterate child that was never taught to read. Unlike X's father who was chosen to be part of a large family of devotees, most of us remained orphans to our own spirits.

X and I talked about other things: about the way she moved, about her cats and how the pandemic had been so overwhelming for the both of us. "Has your father seen you move?" I asked as I stretched myself out on the carpet, delighted that I felt this ease around her. "No. My parents don't know that I do this. I've been living this double life thing for a long time. Like my dad," she said almost immediately, then laughed at what she had revealed. "My mom made sure we had good education but it caused an unintended rift between us. Like our life experiences are different from his maybe, the way we were brought up is different from how he was brought up. And that made us distanced."

That night as I left her studio, I thought about multiplicities of selves, stories, and lives. I thought about the Ganesha idols, all of them in different sizes, coming from different places, worshipped by different individuals and ending up on that rack. These idols were carried by the same sea that extinguished the paper boats that brought me here to X. I thought about my mother who had been adopted and how parts of me came from that absence. My mother had met and kept in touch with her biological mother and her half-siblings but none of them resembled her. My mother and I were multiple selves of a ghost man we would never meet. Or maybe we had met, each time my skin folded into itself, when I sensed the echoes of the land or when the quiver danced inside me.

(iv)

Cik Man, can I ask you something? How do you know when is a good day to fish?

Oh. You just need to look at the sky to know. You see how the clouds are sparse and far apart right now? That means there is not much fishes. Sometimes when you go out at around 5 p.m. and the sky's a little reddish, that means you'll catch a lot of prawns. When the clouds look like ikal mayang, like my hair and it sways this way and that way, it means the sea has an abundance of fish. We used to tie a stone to our fishing line and threw it out in the middle of the sea. When we pulled it up, the stone must be warm to touch. If it's cold, we know it's going to be a waste of time and the catch will be quite small. I learn all these from my family. As kids we just ikut-ikut and do not ask so many questions.

"Tunggu. Tunggu dulu."

Do you have children?

I do! She's turning four this December.

You can take my advice if you want to but it's ok if you don't. Don't bother lavishing your child with money and wealth. But do make sure they have the education they need and they will be ok. Insyallah.

How many children do you have, Cik Man?

I have four children. All of them are doing well. My daughter, the third one, is a doctor at a clinic in Punggol.

That's nice, Cik Man. Cik Man, does any one of your four kids follow you on your fishing trips?

Hahaha, of course not. They won't understand it. To them, it's going to be too hot and a waste of time.

So none of your children ever asked you about fishing, or the sea or any of these things you've shared with me?

No, not really. I don't see how it will be of any use to them.

Ah, that's alright, Cik Man. Maybe it's not meant for them.

*

The smell of jasmine, sandalwood, and turmeric permeated the air as she rubbed her skin in circular motions, harnessing the energies in her maternal body, and scraping it off into a viscous mass of skin, dirt, and a longing borne from her loneliness.

She gently caressed the mass with her fingers, imagining a young boy with big eyes, curly hair and a little baby belly before kissing him on the lips, breathing life into bone, blood and flesh.

Ganesha, she whispered as he opened his eyes. He was born outside of the womb and existed alongside the cycles of rebirth. As he took in the world and the face of Parvati, his mother and creator, he absorbed the knowledge that existed beyond time and space, beyond the samsara. In a single breath, Ganesha experienced a billion lifetimes before and after his present form, in the arms of Parvati, who was enraptured by this child.

Needing to replenish her maternal energies, Parvati wanted to soak herself in the vast bath of the universe and tasked Ganesha to stand guard at the door, especially for Shiva who had barged in with no notice several times. Parvati did not wish to be disturbed. Ganesha might have already known the events that would follow but knew he could not stop them. Ganesha stood fiercely by the door awaiting his fate.

As Shiva returned from his long meditation in the Himalaya, he came home to an earnest boy guarding the chambers of his wife, refusing to let him in. Not recognising that Ganesha is Parvati's son, he cut off the boy's head for his insolence. The sight of Ganesha's headless body when Parvati came out of the bath sent her into a rage. She threatened to destroy the entire universe unless Shiva brought Ganesha back to life. Shiva found the first living being, an elephant, killing it and severing its head to replace Ganesha's.

Like all the origin stories of the gods and goddess, there are multiple versions of Ganesha's origin story. This version is the one that is widely shared. Reading through each of these stories, I've always wondered if Ganesha's wisdom was acquired only after, from the head of the sacrificed elephant. Or was the wisdom attributable to being born outside of the womb? In almost all of the versions, Shiva beheaded Ganesha because he could not recognise his son. I think of Cik Man and his children, X and her father, and my biological grandfather.

What was severed and what replaced it?

Last time, in Bedok you had all these hills, you know? All the hills were cut and made into earth that stretched the shores of East Coast.

Was there kampong on these hills, Cik Man?

Yes, of course there were. Clustered kampongs on the hills. Bedok used to have beaches too.

Boleh bayangkan tak?

Bayang, I thought to myself. To imagine shadows that are long gone.

I looked at Cik Man for a while, trying to make out his face but knowing that I might not cross paths with him again. Strangely he looked at me and pulled down his mask, so I could see his face.

Going home?

Yes, Cik Man. Thank you for sharing all those wonderful stories with me.

It was my pleasure. Maybe that's why I come here to fish today. It was probably so I would meet you.

(v)

It was really hard to track the exact locations and timings of the sending-off ceremonies. Unlike the other well-known festivals here, the nine emperor gods festival seems to elude access by people outside of the different temples that are practising it. I had caught sight on social media of some of the rituals performed in the last few years, but never encountered them in person. Not until this year, when I found myself caught in some current that kept bringing me back (to where?). Scenes from a short film, the conversation with X, and a recurring dream of burning paper floating in the water.

I cycled out to East Coast to meet Jane, who wanted to document the send-off again this year. We were told by a few people that it was going to be at Carpark F, as it had always been. On my way, I realised there were many parts to Carpark F. I caught sight of the table of offerings placed on the shore as the sun was setting. It was such a beautiful sight and strangely not out of place.

Jane told me that we might want to explore more of Carpark F to find the spot with the largest temple.

Yeah, last time we went to a site which only had one boat. But we kept walking and found a site with more boats. I didn't know why some temples had fewer boats.

You mean all the temples are here tonight?

I'm not sure actually.

So what happens now?

We wait. The last time, it dragged on quite late. But we cannot question the gods and their timing, can we?

Let's not move from here yet then.

There were some members from the temple dressed in white, with a white scarf on their heads. They had their masks on and were standing inside the red and white tape barricading the space for worship. Jane mentioned the tape was added only this year, maybe as part of the safe-distancing measures. As we were waiting, a woman approached us and asked if this was the entourage for the temple in Sengkang. Her mother was part of the entourage and they were on their way from the temple. She received a phone call and told us she was heading towards the end of Carpark F.

About fifteen minutes later, we saw a little boat coming to shore. Jane explained that this boat would be pulling the paper boats out before they were set on fire in the middle of the sea. We saw another boat moving farther down. I turned to Jane, and both of us took it as a second sign to move further down the beach. After walking quite a distance we caught sight of giant floodlights lighting the entire space. Unlike the first place we were at, the barricaded area was twice as large and clusters of people were waiting all around us. There were offerings placed on the sand, but I could not make out what they were. There was also a table of offerings much like the one we saw earlier. Some of the people, who were dressed in white with the same headgear, were burning incense and spearing the burning sticks into the sand. The smoke wafted in the air, merging with the smell of the sea. I felt my body bristling, unsure if it was from seeing all this for the first time or from being awakened.

I turned and caught sight of four boats made of paper, with talismans pasted all over. On the boats were little effigies of the gods themselves. I did not know how much time had passed. In the distance, I caught sight of a single paper boat burning in the sea. It came from the place we were at earlier. Behind it, brighter than the flames, was a cruise ship with giant LED screens spelling out "WE LOVE SINGAPORE".

One of the photographers informed us that the entourage was arriving. Two men came to the edge of the barricade and briefed us on the house rules for the night.

Do not stand in the way of the sedan chairs.

Please do not get too close. Please do not crowd around.

Do give enough room for everyone.

If you are a woman, please do not accidentally touch, it is dangerous if you do.

Everything was said in Hokkien, and again in Mandarin. One of them pointed to me and asked if I understood and started to explain these house rules in Malay. I laughed and wondered how many bystanders had been carelessly treating this as a spectacle, like the National Day or Chingay parades. But to be fair, I felt I was intruding into a sacred space too, just by being there. Slowly as the incense started to waft in thick plumes, I felt my body opening up.

I could hear the cymbals and bells as the procession came into the barricaded area. Moments later several sedan chairs, carried by four men each, were dancing on the shore. Back and forth, side to side, in the water and out again. The chants were whispers from where I was and the devotees started to fill up the area outside the barricade with incense sticks clasped between their palms. They were kneeling facing the sea. I felt a giant cloth had been pulled from the corners of the island, wrapping all of us underneath it. Suddenly all was quiet, except for the waves. We were underwater, buoyant and drowning all at once. I was kneeling too, overwhelmed by the intensity.

The hard claps from the whip broke the silence. One of the mediums was whipping himself, and the chants seemed to be getting louder. I turned to see the arrival of the other paper boats. There were nine of them now. One for each god. Jane told me she would be at the breakwater, and I wandered back to shore. I saw several men kneeling in a row. Their all-white outfits created a high contrast to the orange life jackets they had on. They also wore masks. I had watched the same men earlier, going into the water. They were pulling the paper boats, with the help of the small boat that was parked near the shore. One of the men was carrying a lit torch. Others were running with the urns to be placed in the paper boats. Those who were praying placed their incense in the sand and stood at the shore with me.

The men grew smaller, almost disappearing into the horizon, and I thought to myself, what happens if the fire from the torch burns out? What happens if it rains? What happens if one of the men starts to drown?

I kept thinking too, from the moment I heard it, why not a woman and why is it dangerous?

(vi)

"Water spirits are one of the most vicious spirits," he said, with a look of warning in his eyes.

A devotee explained that there were various types of spirits with different levels of strength and power, but Dou Mu, the heavenly Queen of Heaven and mother of the nine emperor gods, wielded exceptional power as a strong water spirit and therefore was given authority over the seas.

It was no wonder the gods had to be fetched and sent off from their place of origin—a river or sea.

Dou Mu. 斗母元君. She held the knowledge of celestial mysteries, passing through the seas and protecting seafarers. Queen of heaven, with her sixteen arms, two clasped in prayer. One of the origin stories portrayed the nine emperor gods as human sovereigns or monarchs. After gaining enlightenment, Dou Mu imparted her transcendental knowledge to her nine sons, and they became the nine emperor gods, making up the constellation known in the Western world as the Big Dipper.

I sat on the shore for a long time, taking in the sight of the burning boats moving slowly apart. A constellation of flames floated brightly on the sea's surface, unyielding even in the face of the strongest of waves. The tradition itself had lived through several erasures under the guise of modernity and progress, and had been thriving from the devotion of those seeking prosperity and good fortune. I wondered, how many of these devotees were from families of seafarers and migrants who made this place their home many, many years ago? Multiplicities of selves, stories, and lives.

The men were coming back now, their white outfits completely soaked. I thought about my favourite origin story from Songkhla, Thailand, in which a group of fishermen found a vase floating in the sea. They could hear strange voices asking them to remove the talisman paper and unseal the vase. When it was removed, they saw nine heads soaring into the sky in broad daylight. On the same night, one of the fishermen had a dream of the gods forewarning him of an impending storm, but they promised him safety if a flag was erected on the masthead with the words "Jiuhuangye" written on it. The fisherman warned the rest of his crew but they laughed at him in disbelief. After they set sail together, a fierce storm wrecked all the boats and the fishermen drowned. Only the boat with the erected flag survived the calamity.

The remover of obstacles.

I caught sight of Jane on the breakwater and climbed up slowly, feeling reverberations all around me. I could feel you inside me. You were wide awake and I was wide open. I looked behind to see that the space was slowly emptying out. I turned, expecting to see Jane, but she was nowhere to be found. In the stillness, I caught a glimpse of you beside me and I turned, but there was no one. Again I looked out to see the last of the cinders burning out. A bright light flashed upward momentarily and I caught a glimpse of you again, a streak of fleshy pink, as the quiver finally left me.

Jumpa lagi, I say under my breath.

As I walked back down to the shore, I saw Jane still standing at the edge of the breakwater. "You ok?" she asked when she finally joined me. "Never better," I replied and under the darkened skies, I whispered a silent thanks to the currents for bringing me back to where I needed to be.

"EARLY AND LATE" AND "EVERY POET WANTS TO BE YOUR DOG"

Chris Huntington

EARLY AND LATE

One of my students turns in her paper, but she accidentally gives me one for another class too. As a result, the online portal marks her work as EARLY and LATE, which I tell her is how I've felt my entire life. She doesn't laugh because she's nervous and maybe because I'm not funny. Lydia Davis called her book CAN'T AND WON'T which is also a good title, but not for me. I want to tell my student that when I was in seventh grade I joined the track team, and forty years later my father still chuckles about how I came in not just last, but so far behind that the coach waved for me to get off the track so they could get the next racers started. In high school, I had a crush on a girl, but I was afraid to kiss her even when she sat beside me in her running shorts with her chin on her knee. And then I resolved to kiss her, but she took a year abroad. I wanted to wander the earth and now here I am. When my mother was born, there wasn't a term for "Chinese girl born in Dallas," so people just called her a Jap. Years later, I lived in Taiwan where I was asked why I had a nose like a white guy, and I said, "one half," (一半) which is how I described myself because I wasn't fluent. Sometimes I think I can speak English but the feeling passes. In Gabon, I left a woman's house by the back door when unexpected headlights filled the window of her bedroom. I frightened all the chickens in the yard, so it was a terrible getaway, but then again, no one came looking. This was a relief at the time but also like a knife in the heart. I suppose I can laugh about it now, but with whom? My student apologizes again for the mix-up. I smile. How seldom we say what needs to be said. How seldom we can. I want to tell her: There is nothing to apologize for. All my life I have felt early or late. I want to tell her: Timing is everything when you write a poem. Or tell a joke. You have to know when to be silent.

EVERY POET WANTS TO BE YOUR DOG

Dogs don't see well enough to read, which makes me sad. Dog words would have to move like rabbits, like squirrels, like birds on the white sky of a page. Letters would have to smell like rivers, like old beer cans, like pavement. Dogs are color-blind, too, which makes me sad when I think about all the bright green they miss out on in the spring, but they probably feel the same way about me in the fall, when leaves are burning and the earth is a breezey open hand, a song made of compost and damp bark. Emily Dickinson had a dog named Carlo, who had no idea what a writer was or that she was one. When Carlo died, Dickinson wrote that time was no remedy for her loss, but this wasn't entirely true, of course—because eventually she also died. Time puts an end to everything. Emily Dickinson wrote poems her whole life: faintly, in pencil, on the backs of envelopes hidden in her pocket. I've always been in love with poems, but I am fifty-three and I find poetry to be more and more unreadable. Not because of the language. But because the small presses print the words so small, in thin-armed serif that looks to me like frost on a chain-link fence. Is this how a dog feels? A friend of mine did Shotokon karate for years, so long that his black belt turned the color of chalk. I feel that way about poetry. I feel like all poetry is turning into a white page. All my life, I have been told to say less or maybe even nothing. The world doesn't need my poems. I should find some happiness in this. As I get older, it feels more and more urgent that I go for a walk, even in the rain. The world is waiting.

I AM WAITING FOR AN APOLOGY.

Rachel Kuanneng Lee

CW: Suicide

(I think it's going to be a long wait.)
Since you're here in the kitchen
waiting with me,

why not I tell you
a secret or
two? You see, we don't

know each other
very well, and I've developed a weakness
for telling secrets

to strangers.

*

Secret: My younger sister killed herself.

These days, I want
to start every conversation
with that statement. I can trace

this feeling back to its
beginning:
I felt the desire bloom

on the edge
of the pavement where I stood with the plainclothes police officer.
"If there's anything else you think

might help with the investigation, or if you have
any questions,
you have my number," he says.

Motioning to leave now, his hands are full with zip-lock bags
of her belongings. "Wait," I am teetering,
"Her friends. They would want to know."

He fishes for her phone in a zip-lock, gives
me the number of the friend she last
texted, to whom she had said

nothing of her plans:

The rope she'd bought, from which I'd earlier
cut her stiff neck. Her phone left
passwordless, from which I now

get a phone number. And then, there is no secret. The wake
is a three-day affair. Her friends tell more friends,
and they come, and they come some more.

One collapses beside her open casket. One paces
the parlor, reads the dedications
others have earlier written, sits and

talks with old classmates, stays
till midnight, drives another home, comes
back the next day, and then

approaches her body. It is a face
painted several shades too dark—to mask the blue—
a skin-tight dress in flowers of white and orange

distending gently at the stomach. It is falsies I buy
at the nearest Watson's on the first morning,
when my mother weeps at the trauma

death brings to her daughter's lash extensions. The funeral director
calls the undertaker back to affix the two black fans
onto lids whose eyes do not see—

but it must be done.

My mother insists.
And she is right. You only need
see the result to know—after all, my sister would not

have wanted to be seen ugly, only dead. But come back
to the boy—he holds her small hand, warm from every
body's aching grasp.

One brings flowers. Another, too.
They all bring flowers, although my sister
will tell you she hates

receiving flowers. They die.
She does not know
what to do with them,

but what you give up in exchange for choosing
your death is the ability to shape
this story.

*

And so, there is no secret.
There isn't one because I
have decided there won't be one.

In my ideal world, I begin
each conversation after her death with
"My sister killed herself,"

and maybe I become
the one who outrageously overshares or
the one who would

use suicide to call attention
to herself.
If I were trying

to get you to like me,
neither of those is a good
place to be,

but you see, stranger,
that really isn't
what I want.

*

Secret: Earlier this year, I started thinking a lot about Wilfred Owen again.

I get to know Owen over two years, through
critical analysis in English Literature class of a slim
book of collected poems. In the Faber & Faber,

we streak lines like streamers, marking
pages now browned from the edges.
I am seventeen and

eighteen and living
in the most affluent city in Southeast Asia.
What do I know of war?

The Japanese occupation, the British
abandonment, all pieces put together to reason
my country's Enlistment Act, the propaganda

reel in the cinema, where I appear
the smiling girlfriend, wife, mother.
Not shown, of course, the ones who touch men torn

of war "like some queer disease", or men
who return to find all doors shut to them, or the boys
whose blades "keen with the hunger of blood".

On a sticky afternoon, we split
the book down to "Apologia Pro Poemate Meo".
An arrow curves

from title to margin, where we pencil "(An) Apology
for My Poetry". Then, in greater gray scribblings—Owen is NOT
apologizing, NOT sorry. He expresses

no guilt for depicting the horrors of war, or writing
its dull hopelessness. It is not hope
he sees on the battlefield.

He does not seek our forgiveness for turning young men
from war's burnished honors or desire to temper his excoriating ending, "These men are worth
Your tears: You are not worth their merriment",

with regret at his own scorn. We annotate:
in Greek, an "apologia" is a defense—
a justification. What Owen wants

is to convince us that the sight of someone "guttering, choking,
drowning", their "drooping tongues", "chasms round
their fretted sockets" makes at least sufficient case

against the glory of dying,
even if for your country. And I promise you,
there is no glory left

in the masks
of the dying. You
recoil,

no, I—I recoiled—
when I saw her body in death,
venous, purpled,

bathed in the room's garish orange lamplight.
"Move him into the sun", says Owen's speaker,
"If anything might rouse him now

The kind old sun will know."
I want to be the sort of person who shrieks a solar flare into existence.
Instead, for a precious few

seconds, I freeze. I
freeze and I say to myself,
"Is there any way we can please not-see this?"

At the cusp
of the eclipse, just before
the sun turns dark,

the speaker begs, "Please".
She spins around on her heel, willing herself to
stay—walk away—stay. Please.

*

Is this a better way
to tell a secret? If I do it this way,
do you ask yourself

who Wilfred Owen is? Do you wonder
if he is my first
boyfriend? For a moment, do you

think maybe I'm still hung
up over him?
Can't expect everyone to know

a First World War poet, no matter my
personal inclinations. Those of you who do know
might be torn

between the curiosity of the connection and the
minor irritation that I should drag
this dead white man

into this. But the familiarity—
does it endear you to me for a while? Enough that maybe
when the poem draws on,

you'll be the ones
who'll listen when I open my mouth and each time
out spills my dead sister—her pale

body plastic-wrapped, lids fallen back
to blood-laced whites. Nearer you, a foot arched out,
the big toenail cracked burgundy.

"I need you to . . . " "—yes", you
hear the words said, "I confirm that this is my
sister."

*

Secret: I'm sorry about the oranges I once dropped in front of a Buddhist altar.

The oranges are Sunkist, which really means
it isn't my fault, because unlike mandarins
that are flat-topped, these

are round. Consider this
a twofold apology, as in "I'm sorry I dropped the oranges", but also
"I had a very good reason for dropping these oranges". I mean,

they stack four round fruit in a pyramid
and you're supposed to hold it and bow—a sign of respect for the dead, an invitation
to eat in this syncretic jumble of Chinese-Singaporean-Buddhist tradition, except

in most situations, it is younger folk who perform this
100th-day commemoration rite for those older than them.
In that moment, when I should have been thinking

about balancing oranges, I was thinking about kiwis.
A hundred days and two weeks before,
my sister makes a new Instagram account.

It is public-facing,
to celebrate the small,
daily

joys.

There are a total of eight posts.
She captions one, her brow furrowed, eyes squinting in the afternoon sun, simply
"I loved today". Another

at my octogenarian aunt's, slide one:
her, smiling at the camera, pretending
to rearrange a fridge magnet. Two: a back view

of me in Lunar New Year red dress, looking at the same set
of magnets. Three: selfie. Me (left), her (right).
Four: a family photo. Five: a still

from the movie *Soul*. This series she captions
"One day I'll have my own
sun-drenched old lady kitchen, where I'll eat

a kiwi over the sink
while looking out the window
[Kissy face, no heart eyes] [Half kiwi]".

For several years, my own WhatsApp status reads,
"still desires kiwi fruit".
We speak in obtuse angles

about one day making an indie movie with a scene
where the protagonist in an oversized t-shirt and boyshorts cuts
a kiwi in half, stands over

the kitchen sink and eats it, spoon by spoon.
Green kiwi juice in little spurts everywhere. Camera pans out
and then we see

a contented smile play across her lips.
"Thus their heads wear this hilarious, hideous,
Awful falseness of set-smiling corpses",

says Owen's speaker in "Mental Cases". If you look
at the posts framing her likeness,
is that how you should see them? False?

Me? I don't know.
Before the wake, my brother coordinates
an effort to memorialize her. Her best friend gathers photographs

and you see her—smiling out
from every single one. No kiwis
in sight but the first time

she tries to kill herself I am wearing a kiwi-green calf-length skirt, my first
day at a new job. It is a good day. I get home,
open the door to my room and

find her sitting
in a puddle of her own puke.
A mug of brown liquid, a packet

of twenty-four pills dispensed by the mental
health institute emptied at the bed's foot.
Dazed,

she refuses to speak to anyone but me.
Her small damp fingers grasping mine, "You don't
understand. . . . I'm not supposed to be here,

I was supposed to die," she whispers.
And four years

later, she does finally
succeed, and I
standing stupidly

askew of the altar,
I think how, for all the sharp colors
pin-pressed into my mind, this is

the only apology I receive.

And so, I
drop the oranges—they should have
been kiwis anyway.

*

For ten months, I've told this secret. "I'm sorry,"
I begin. One time, with a trigger
warning. Another time I say,

"This is a horrific thing and I know you'll feel bad
for me once I say it, but several
months have passed and I'm

okay now." Each time, I make
to begin somewhere else and to go
someplace different. Each time,

I apologize. Maybe today instead, I will stick

my hands into the secret and try to cut it open
to something different. I watched a video where a man slices
an apple diagonally across—upper right

to lower left—it was enough for me to
buy a chef's knife so I, too,
can scallop my apples into swans. It made me think,

heck, if I watch enough videos, maybe I could carve
all my fruits and vegetables
into some kind of brilliant animal. I could

whittle a kiwi until I see seed but think
death. Or I could slice it in half and
hand one off to you, stranger.

The spoon is in the topmost drawer
underneath the sink. I am waiting
for my apology. Will you wait

with me?

WHAT IT WANTS

Minxi Chua

She realizes it's missing on Wednesday morning.

Standing at the bathroom mirror, glasses askew, toothbrush in her right hand. The left holds her phone, WhatsApp messages from her boss crowding the screen. *Need you to stay late tonight, Xinyi.* It's 6:48a.m.; the sun will be rising soon. She types a reply: *kk can.* Her left thumb, unused to the exercise, cramps. Pain shoots down the inside of her forearm, a white-hot needle threading her nerves. Xinyi rolls her wrist, grimacing. The problem needs fixing, she knows. She'll get around to it, eventually.

Her bathroom mirror is steamed up from the shower, but she doesn't bother cleaning it. What's there to look at? She doesn't wear makeup or jewellery. Just a pair of silver stud earrings she's had since primary school. Plus the tinted ChapStick in her handbag Cora bought her two or three birthdays ago. It tastes like cherries, dipped in chemicals, but she never goes a day without it.

6:52 a.m. Xinyi spits in the sink, clamps the phone under her chin, shimmies into her pants. Her fingers feel weak from the spasm, uncoordinated, like those of a very small child's. She struggles with the buttons, mumbles mild curses under her breath, looks down to adjust herself—looks down—

That's when she realizes—it's gone.

Her phone falls, skidding across the tiles.

She touches her chest, fingers slightly trembling.

Between her breasts, the window of transparent skin, as tall and wide as her open hand, stretched taut like clingfilm over cloudy muscle, the colour and opacity of barley water. Nothing out of the ordinary there. She sweeps both palms across the familiar plane, counting off her visible ribs in Cantonese, a habit from childhood: yat, yee, saam, sei. The rib cage extends from the breastbone, and encases her lungs like a cocoon, protecting the wet, elastic organs, which she watches fill and empty even as her breathing grows uneven. Ribs, sternum, lungs. Next, the heart.

Her heart should be plain to see, tucked in its usual spot on the left side of the chest, thumping to keep her alive. But where is it now? She straightens her glasses, wipes down the mirror and stares into it. Maybe she's made a mistake. Imagined an absence where none can exist. But her reflection, unchanged in every other way, does not lie. The heart. Where is the heart?

Her heart is gone.

"Shit," Xinyi mutters.

Then she kneels, dazed and shivering, to pick up her phone.

Checks the time: 7:04 a.m. Peter has sent another text: *Meeting moved up to 7:15—get here now!*

Nestled amid his demands, a message from Cora: *OMG uk work visa just came thru! LONDON HERE I COME!* and one from her older brother: *r u gonna miss dinner next week 2? mom & dad r pissed :/*

"Shit." Xinyi slicks back her hair. Puts on the bra and blouse hanging on the bathroom door. Takes a few slow, measured breaths. In five minutes, she's out the door and off to work; only getting home that night after ten, too tired to think, let alone stress out over anatomy. She falls asleep in her office clothes, dreaming of nothing.

+++

Thursday, 6:30 a.m. Xinyi wakes to her phone alarm: still tired, a bit stiff, but not dead.

It shouldn't be possible, to be without a heart. At the office, she does some idle Googling: *heart has gone missing; can't see heart in chest; how to get my heart back?* She skims articles on health sites like *Psychocardio Today*; scours lifestyle blogs; even consults a few conspiratorial videos on YouTube, where skeletal white women in low-cut tops claim that eating only fruit for six months "can combat sudden heartlessness, as well as its related symptoms, like low moods, low energy, and of course, the dreaded weight gain."

Briefly, she contemplates asking her friends for advice, or even her family. Then she remembers the last time she told her mother she was ill—how her mother insisted she move back into their family's HDB apartment until she recovered, guilting her every time she showed signs of improvement, since she would soon be "abandoning" the family again. The thought of sitting alone in her childhood bedroom is enough to ensure her silence. Plus, most of her friends she knows from work—personal issues of this nature hardly pass for decent office banter. So she tells no one.

The week passes without incident. *Perhaps*, Xinyi thinks, *everything is fine. I just need to put my head down, work hard, and get on with it.* Still, sometimes, an entirely different thought crosses her mind. *I wish I could get naked with someone.* She wishes she could undo their buttons, strip them down, and inspect what's ticking away underneath. It's been years since she's laid eyes on another human heart up close.

The last one belonged to her then-boyfriend; the one Cora called "Norman", though that was not his name: "Because he's such a *normie!*" He was an uncomplicated man, friendly and clear-chested. They'd met in university, dated for six years, and broken up in a Marina Bay Sands hotel suite, because she refused to marry him. That entire night, he kept asking her: "What is it you really want, Xinyi?"

Again and again he asked, even as she answered: *I want to buy my own HDB. I want a promotion in the next five years. I want my parents to get the hell off my back.* Standard, irreproachable responses. Yet they seemed only to upset him further, until, finally, he relented: "I can give you everything you say you want, but it'll never be enough, will it?"

He had started crying then, naked in bed beside her, and she'd found him unbearable to look at. But she wishes now she had observed him more closely, especially during sex. Now, she can barely recall the details of his face, let alone the most intimate part of his body.

Yet what good would it do to witness the heart of another? What could it change?

Can she stick her fist through someone's skin, rummage around in their viscera, and extract the core of their being to replace her own? Impossible. Then again, it's impossible that she still draws breath; that she can take the MRT to work, write reports for investors, eat Shin Ramen at her desk, shit, move, think thoughts, ignore aches, and do all the million other things that constitute being alive, mechanically speaking. Maybe this is the trick to life. You get on with it, even when it stops making sense. You care less about what you want, focus only on what you can get, until you finally stop caring at all, and let the days churn on, steady as a heartbeat.

+++

Then Cora comes over for Sunday dinner.

They don't see each other as often as they used to. Xinyi is always busy with work; Cora with whatever or whoever she happens to be doing at the moment. But they had been best friends in junior college: the Twisted Sisters, except they were both wild-maned Asians with bad attitudes. During recess, they would cover their arms in Sharpie tattoos, competing to see who could don the most daring design: a hairy vulva, an upside-down cross, a swastika.

Once, in Xinyi's bedroom after school, they took off their pinafores and drew flowers on each other's chests. Xinyi remembers weaving black vines between the lines of Cora's ribs: yat, yee, saam, sei; remembers Cora's soft, fluttering laughter when Xinyi would press down too hard with her pen: "*Ah*, it tickles!" They sat side by side on Xinyi's mattress, a hand-me-down from her older brother. The worn, springy foam still smelled pungently of teenage boy, and gave her lower back pain; still, sitting there with Cora, Xinyi had never felt more at ease. But her heart remained hidden under her bralette, as did Cora's; those glassy panes of secret flesh never fully exposed.

As adults, only Cora has maintained a proclivity for art and inked skin. She's also a social-justice activist now, and a bisexual. She signs petitions to get drug dealers off death row, goes to Pink Dot rallies with Priya, her "heart partner", and complains endlessly about everything.

Tonight, her gripe of choice is income inequality:

"But why *should* fund managers get paid so much? All you do is move people's money around."

"You *know* it's more than that. Peter says I'll be up for a leadership role next quarter."

"Peter works you like a dog, Xinyi. You know, this is why I can't stand this country. People put up with so much bullshit! Once Pri and I get out of here, we're never coming back."

"Not this again, Cora." Xinyi suspects that she is Cora's token "normie" friend; less a real human being, and more a topic she can whip out at parties, to use as both scapegoat and punchline: *Look at Xinyi, she represents everything that's wrong with Singapore! She votes PAP in every election, and she only wears panties her mother buys for CNY! Loser alert!*

Usually, such a thought would rile Xinyi into righteous anger: *If I'm such a loser, then why are you too broke to buy your own dinner?* But she can no longer muster the strength to react. For one thing, work's been tiring; for another, her heart's been missing for weeks, and she's convinced it's not coming back.

Some mornings, she wakes up feeling so drained, wrung so dry of purpose, that she must draw on every drop of willpower within herself to get her blood pumping again. Otherwise, she may not get out of bed at all. She was half an hour late to work last Monday. Peter dressed her down in front of the whole department, but worse than that was the fact it barely bothered her.

"Okay." Cora stares at her, pierced eyebrow raised. "What's up with you?"

"Nothing. Do you want dessert? The bingsu place stops delivering after nine."

"Stop it," Cora snaps, suddenly stern. "You know I hate it when you switch off like that. I know you're not telling me something. Come on, spill!"

Briefly, Xinyi thinks she may lie, or distract her with a few insults: *What's wrong? How about your fake-ass relationship? Or does Priya still think you'll want kids some day, or that you actually like Indian food?* Then the fatigue kicks in again, and instead she thinks: *Why bother denying it?*

"My heart is gone."

This time, Cora's laughter is loud and startled. "What?"

"It's gone. I woke up one morning and took a look at myself and it was just gone. At first, I thought I was going psycho, but lately I feel my pulse slowing down, and sometimes I can't hear my heartbeat anymore. Don't worry about it, though. I'll get it sorted out."

"Sure." Cora's expression is unreadable. As children, they had looked so similar that people often assumed they were related. Xinyi had found this funny, but Cora hated it, loudly and proudly, for reasons she could not, or perhaps would not, articulate. Though by the time she grew out of this strange hostility, the problem was moot. They had grown into two different women: Cora becoming more beautiful by the year, Xinyi more boring. Sometimes, just looking at Cora feels like an act of profound self-loathing. Xinyi must avert her eyes, or else be overcome by unease, a tightening at the pit of her gut, like hunger pangs.

"You don't believe me."

"I *do*!" Even as she says this, Cora shakes her head. "It's just . . . are you okay?"

"I told you, I'll get it sorted out. I've just been really busy lately."

"Right." For a few minutes, Cora says nothing else. Instead, she pulls out her phone, and starts scrolling. The silence comforts Xinyi. Transports her back to that old bedroom; to those warm, hushed hours hidden inside its walls, where happiness was measured in private pleasures, whispers, glimpses of white bone and blue vein in the afternoon sun. Then her phone chimes, and she is here again: twenty-eight, living alone in an overpriced rental, too exhausted to even feel miserable.

"I just sent you a phone number," Cora says. "And I want you to promise me something, okay? For my going-away present. No expensive chocolates this time, or designer bags I'll never use."

All Xinyi can do is nod. By now, it's getting late. She's got to be up at 6:30 a.m. tomorrow; Cora's flight to England is in less than a week.

"Great!" Cora's grin is brilliant, affectionate. "Promise me you'll make an appointment with the woman whose number I gave you. She's super nice, a total professional. Priya says she's politically open-minded too, even though she's straight, cis and Chinese."

"Fine," Xinyi sighs. "She's a sis? You mean she's a nun or something?"

"Cis. As in cisgender?" Cora sighs even louder, and shakes her head again, her long, straight hair swaying like a bolt of silk. She looks like Zhang Ziyi in *House of Flying Daggers*, the killer rebel playing blind; she looks like one of the old ink paintings in the Lee Kong Chian Art Museum, a portrait of some artist's muse: to be forever adored at arm's length, yet never again touched, her inner workings never again to be seen, in their grotesque, fleeting beauty. "Forget it. I've told you enough times already."

Xinyi watches her turn to stare out the window, her gaze wistful and distant, as though in search of somewhere to land. Some faraway place where explanations are no longer needed, and understanding another person is as easy as listening to their voice, looking into their eyes, and pressing the see-through skin of your chest against their own, heart-to-heart.

+++

She makes an appointment with Priya's doctor that Tuesday. She does this indifferently, feeling none of the embarrassment that such a situation should warrant. Perhaps this is the lone upside to heartlessness: an immunity to humiliation. She is even unfazed by the fact that Priya makes more money than her—if the exorbitant cost of the appointment is anything to go by. *Or maybe*, Xinyi thinks, *she's one of those fancy Indians, whose family makes all the tyres in Eastern Europe or something. Is that better than selling out, Cora? Not all of us can be born so free and lucky.*

"So why is it you're here to see me today, Xinyi?"

"My heart is gone." She grimaces, as Dr. Tan jots down a note on her iPad. Though the office is spacious, located in a quiet, discreet corner of Holland Village, Xinyi cannot help but feel claustrophobic. Like she is a child again, stuck in her bedroom; like her mother might barge in at any moment and catch her in the act. "I'm only here as a favour to a friend, though. I don't really believe in therapists."

Dr. Tan looks up from her notes and smiles, in a manner that Xinyi cannot help but interpret as teasing, perhaps even condescending. "That's a very common response amongst first-time patients, Xinyi. Unfortunately, there's still plenty of stigma in our country around Major Acardiognosic Disorder, as well as other psychocardiac disorders. It doesn't help that the government is constantly telling us to cover up our chests, in the name of 'public decency'. Still, with the right combination of therapies and medication, MAD can be very treatable nowadays. It's nothing to be ashamed about."

"I'm not ashamed," Xinyi rebuts. "Just confused."

"You want to know why this is happening to you. I hear that a lot too."

"So?" Xinyi fidgets in her seat. The armchair she sits in is comfortable enough, its plush cushions freshly dry-cleaned and lavender-scented. Yet she cannot relax into it, cannot find a position or placement that suits her here. "What is it then? Tell me what's wrong with me."

To her chagrin, Dr. Tan shifts in her chair as well, mirroring even the way Xinyi crosses her legs. "Well, Xinyi, MAD can be caused by a number of factors. Work stress, for example. Traumatic childhood experiences and romantic relationships are also common. Sometimes, the disorder is preceded by a long-standing issue, like an identity crisis, or maybe a feeling of overwhelming loneliness. Then there are times when it corresponds to one specific event, like losing a loved one, or even moving to a new country. Tell me, Xinyi, do any of these examples sound familiar to you?"

"No." The conversation does not go much further than this. Dr. Tan asks questions about her family, her love life; Xinyi gives short, factual responses. Once the hour is up, Dr. Tan shakes her hand.

"Well done today, Xinyi. Let's meet same time next week?"

"Maybe," Xinyi murmurs. "Sometimes I have to work through lunch."

That night, she thinks nothing more of the session, or the wry slant of Dr. Tan's smile.

Instead, she dreams. Dreams of Norman, the ugly, meaty smell of him; the way she would screw her eyes shut when he fucked her, like that could erase his heft atop her, his thin, hairy lips nibbling at her breasts. Dreams of the day she got her ears pierced; the Poh Heng shopgirl pinning her to the chair as she wept, gun to her head; her brother laughing, her mother half-soothing, half-scolding: "Don't you want to look pretty like all the other girls?" Dreams of the time her mother caught her and Cora with the Sharpies, their white blouses strewn across her bedroom floor.

The memory replays in her head as she wakes, unbidden thoughts flashing.

The rattan cane held overhead. The red, swollen welts striping her thighs.

And most of all, the screaming, loud enough for the whole apartment floor to hear:

"Sei cau hai! Dirty-hearted slut!"

+++

She misses work on Friday, and Cora's farewell party too.

Stays in bed all day, eating pizza in her panties, ignoring Peter's voice mails.

Saturday afternoon, Cora lets herself into the apartment, suitcases in tow.

"Figure I don't need my key anymore," she says, her voice carrying across the living room. Then, more quietly: "And I wanted to see you before I go. Make sure you're okay."

"I'm fine," Xinyi replies. She hadn't realised that the flight was so soon. Where does the time go? There is a box on her dressing table she's been staring at for at least a few hours; a jewellery box, wrapped with a ribbon. Nestled inside, a bespoke necklace, a purple flower pendant strung on a silver chain. *Such a dumb present,* Xinyi thinks. *Does Cora even like violets anymore? They used to be her favourite.*

"You don't sound fine. Did you go see Dr. Tan like I asked? About your . . . *problem*?"

Problem. Something about the way she says it—the gentle, tentative pity—hurts.

The pain forces Xinyi to her feet, the duvet around her slipping to the floor. She walks forward, through the bedroom door and into the living room. She walks without thought or fear, like it's the most natural thing in the world, a bodily function as basic as breathing. She walks until she reaches Cora. She is naked from the neck down, apart from a pair of frilly Hello Kitty underwear. From her pulsing innards to her dark, puckered nipples, she is completely exposed.

Cora's eyes are wide. Her mouth hangs slightly open.

She's never looked more stupid; she's never looked more beautiful.

Then, for the first time in their lives, Xinyi breaks the silence between them:

"Look at me, Cora. I'm fine. You can see that for yourself, can't you? Come on. Come closer. Why won't you come take a closer look, Cora? Maybe the bloody thing is still inside me. Maybe you'll even find it. Please. Look at me? I'm right here in front of you."

"I can't," Cora stammers. She takes a panicked step back, nearly tripping over the coffee table. When she speaks again, she sounds furious: "I can't do this. What the fuck is *wrong* with you, Xinyi?"

Again, that agony. Except it is no longer confined to her wrist, or her pride; no, it lacerates her all over. Pierces her bared chest like a lightning bolt, a gunshot, a steel bar. It hurts like it might kill her. Like that rattan cane has flayed her most intimate flesh again. Cora is picking up her bags, hissing as she strides out the door: "You had to drop this on me today? Today of all days? All these years we've known each other, and you had to wait until now? When I'm the happiest I've ever been with someone else?"

Her final words to Xinyi are: "And you know what the funny thing is? I *do* see you. I always have. But I can't wait around for you to see *yourself.* Not anymore. You need to figure out what you want out of life on your own, whatever the fuck that is. I'll call when Pri and I are settled in London."

After she's gone, Xinyi stands alone in her apartment: for how long, she isn't sure.

All she sees is the empty room. All she feels are the tears on her face. And all she hears—deep within her chest cavity, amid the gore and horror of her, the tangled web of capillaries and smothered desires—is a throbbing, loud and sure, proving that she is, despite it all, still alive.

"SOUNDPROOF COUNSELING ROOM FOR MIDDLE SCHOOLERS (2009)," "RIPE," AND "RAINING ON MANMULSANG ROCKS (2014)"

Jackson Minjoon Wright

SOUNDPROOF COUNSELING ROOM FOR MIDDLE SCHOOLERS (2009)

reclaim your name

she said

reclaim chin or liu

or whatever it is

and visit vietnam or china

and buy a buddha

she said

even though

my last name

is Scottish so

it's your own fault

for taking martial arts

as a child and playing violin

from such a young age

and also because

you were allergic

to dairy and penicillin

and diamonds. and i

agreed heartily then

filled out evaluations

over takeout.

RIPE

picked
still wet from morning dew
stem clutching dirt for
last bits of knowledge
gained from the

farmer's boot. blinded
for days, binded in a roving
greenhouse—force fed, not
nourished. at the

market, no room to
twitch but time to
rage. on view for you
to buy, cut, burn
just for prestige
mac n' cheese.

rolled off and down the aisle
forgotten amidst the rancid
sound. no notice of
the flesh beneath
your feet. boy

with hungry
pockets. it feels nice
to be embraced
by dirty hands,
again.

smuggled away,
relieved of fluorescence,
and public presence. welcomed
for hardiness and color, but
when this sweetness gives way
to bitterness and the meat

wrinkles into itself, the
seed can travel further still;
new clay pot.

from beneath the soil

blue notes of the pianet
in the other room. fallen
hair on the topsoil brushed
away at the onset
of germination.
breaking through.
sunlight, for once.

bask.

RAINING ON MANMULSANG ROCKS (2014)

Inspired by artwork from Shin Jangsik

A waste of color
to describe wind
in anything but

black and white.
I fell
off of a pine tree,

crashed into Christmas
and baseball diamonds.
I thank

Delta SkyMiles
for free peanuts
and a pacifier

and my only
hanbok.
Behind the mountain

I saw all you painters
drop your palette.
did I lie to the stork

when I told him
where to pick me up?
You all say

No.

"QUEEN," "HOOKUP APP," AND "HOMECOMING"

Daniel W.K. Lee

QUEEN

I was groomed to want
headless white bodies
along men's underwear aisles
in discount department stores.
Long before the world's imagination
got between Marky Mark
and his Calvins, an off-brand
athletic thong modeled
in grayscale dilated these eyes.
Was it all a blur or that hip
meeting upper thigh just the Great Plains
of pelvis for public view?

For a boy in the early chunky years,
would I one day swell
and cast such a chest?
Could I too fill the pouch
to breathlessness?
For a boy with no allowance,
how did I end up deflated
in a red pair of my own,
looking nothing like my lust—
that chessboard display
of the decapitated
sunned to harvest wheat.

Yesteryear's is today's

is tomorrow's window shopping.

Hookup app on any street, alley, or aisle.

Only white guys get away with

parading   cum gutters

in squared touchscreen.

Same game, different board.

Like a queen, I slide in all directions

in conquest—

even over those pale pawns

erased above the chin

I swear

—swore—

need to be more.

HOOKUP APP

If I were
actually headless,

just torso and below
rendered chiseled
and convincing
by bathroom light,
maybe the onlookers
would let the porno
unfold: genuflecting

between
my knees; tongues
taking the host;
my ass: the cathedral
they crave entrance;

and like heaven
depends on it,
pretend

that upon the tap—
this face avowed—
the hard-ons don't die
at the wink

of an almond eye.

HOMECOMING

after *The Hanging Garden*

Do the bluets still bloom below
where I left our adolescence dangling
like a wind chime from the backyard tree?

Someone waiting for blossoms must have said,
"Some things never change," watched
Sweet William's variegated eyes open in June—

after all, that's how we got our name.
Remember? Mountain laurel climbed the sky
in August, not September; Papi backhanded

our mistaken cheeks, letting tears water the rosemary,
but then traded them for ice cream—
two scoops their bribe's worth.

You stayed hung there, overseeing the garden
with your irises shuttered, in your best
and only suit—the crimson shirt still crisp

like winter and the grief clipping your breath
like a sun-dried leaf. All that embalming pain is how
you've stayed unspoiled—even with Papi's sobbing

a messy penance at your navel—
since I martyred you to barter for
something, somewhere else, worth living for.

You, unbearably fourteen, obese with resignation
and our secret bruises: before I leave this house
of wasted perennials, I will bury you.

Everyone else loved you far too much to free
the noose and lay you down like a seed, feared
discovering a failure to furnish roots in this soil.

Do not be afraid, young man, you have long not been living.
And when you are finally under this ground,
we won't care when flowers grow.

A HANDFUL OF LAND

Ayesha Khan

On the day of the first monsoon shower, five-month-old Zébun smiled for the first time. The infant had shown no signs of emotion till that day. When the newborn was passed from one pair of adult hands to the next, it did not so much as let out a shriek or a cry. For the next few months, the baby bore no expressions. She did not whine when hungry. Not a single tear was shed. No baby tantrums to seek attention of the elders. She lay in her cradle, motionless, with eyes that never seemed to blink. Through long eyelashes that curled at the ends, her gaze penetrated the ceiling and the sky above, and seemed to be fixed somewhere in an infinity. Only occasionally did her hands flutter, her legs kick, and the cradle rock, as if to ward off the perils of existence. The parents gaped in horror, the aunts whispered whispers, the uncles hushed hushes. The children waved their hands over her eyes to see if she would trace the motion. The dai brought in kohl made from burnt almonds. But even when the black greasy substance was smeared in her eyes, they refused to blink. The parents secretly wondered if the child would begin to speak late, or ever at all. The grandparents decreed that these were bad omens, signs of some curse perhaps. The aunts clung to their whispers, the uncles to their hushed tones. The children circled the baby in wonder. And when all had despaired and the house lay still on a hot June afternoon, the child smiled. As the rain fell, first a drizzle and then building up to a heavy downpour, perhaps too heavy for a first day rain of the season, the child let out squeals of laughter. A scent of moist soil from the backyard took over the house. The deeper the water seeped into the soil, the more overpowering the scent became. By the evening, it had reached every corner of the house. In the kitchen, it mixed with that of spices. In the old woman's room, it mingled with the sharp fragrance of itr and in the guest room, it stayed on the fresh flowers in the vases. The scent crept under the child's cradle, rocked it to and fro and the child smiled. And chuckled. And laughed. It made its way into her tiny nostrils. For the first time, Baby Zébun showed signs of vitality. The elders assumed it was the rain that had brought the welcome change. The oldest of the house decreed it was indeed the rains—the water from the heavens. It was a cure for all human ailments, they said. And so, no one suspected that the soil had had any role in it. The house had stirred to life. Its residents rejoiced. Glances of relief and nods of approval were exchanged, Zébun's laughter celebrated.

Zébun was the first child born to a couple nearing their forties. There had been debates and arguments as to what the child was to be named. Books with lists of Arabic names were brought out. Maulanas consulted. The names already taken by members of their extended family crossed out. And names of dead ancestors recalled. Zébun's great-grandmother had been a fastidious woman, constantly complaining of specks of dust getting collected in the corners of her room and on the windowsills. She cleaned the kitchen meticulously. She afforded no signs of dust anywhere, no specks of it on her glasses and none in the backyard. Zébun was named after her.

Zébun's childhood days were all alike. She grew up being scolded and chided when found in the backyard with her little fingernails scratching the earth. Nobody, who saw her growing, remembered seeing her nibbling on anything but lumps of earth. Flakes and lumps, and handfuls of it between meals too. The photographs, her childhood preserved in them, showed a plump, fair child with soil all over the mouth. Each day, as the adult world got caught in the web it had spun for itself, Baby Zébun would sneak out unnoticed. She made her way to the backyard and without making a sound, dutifully resumed her routine of feeding on the moist soil. She devoured lumps of earth like they were mashed potatoes. And so by the time she was five, the only food the child knew was the soil from the kitchen garden.

It was the child's only food. It made up all her meals which were to be taken at fixed hours each day. She would be seen crawling out on her knees in broad daylight, sitting under the sun and chewing mouthfuls of earth. She would do the same in the afternoons irrespective of the weather. Rains never deterred her. The sun never bothered. It was food after all, it had to be toiled for. As the day darkened, the first call of Magrib would be an indication to leave her dolls on the mat and sneak out. The child did this with such religiosity that many theories were proposed to explain the unusual habit. The relatives intervened, the extended family suggested a list of *hakims*, the neighbours passed worried glances. Zébun was only talked of in subdued tones with disapproving nods. There were speculations. And prophecies. And heresies. And rumours.

Whoever remembered Baby Zébun remembered a child with a round face, cherry-red lips and a mouth always telling that she had recently dug another hole in the backyard. As she grew, the holes became pits. She shovelled mud out with much ease. Her appetite increased, her pace of digging out the land knew no bounds and the skin around the mouth grew browner than ever. Anyone who was to look at her would think the child probably had a birthmark on her face; that she was perhaps born with a brown patch of skin around the mouth. It was not anything like the black dot mark on every child's cheek meant to protect from nazar or the evil eye, or the prayer bump on the foreheads of devout men. It was rather more like a prominent feature of her face. On days with a cleaner mouth, Baby Zébun looked unusual, almost unnatural. It seemed as if by carrying around that brown patch on her face, the child had marked the kitchen garden as her territory, as if she was claiming the small piece of land as hers, for she had toiled on it each day.

Even after the kitchen garden was gone, concreted over with cement, the girl found ways to hammer her way through the thick layer of cement into the earth. Concealed beneath the hardened grey substance lay the brown soil, pure and untouched. The cement would be scraped off, the stones removed, the good earth dug out, hands filled and the mouth dirtied. Even when the azaans were no longer to be heard and the loudspeakers had been silenced, Zébun's pilgrimage-like expeditions to the backyard did not stop. Nothing puzzled the child. No adult guided her. She needed no reminders to eat. The elders did not cajole her into eating like they did with the other children. It was as though the child heard a voice each day at fixed hours and knew it was time to eat. And so when the house shook with sounds of wailing children and cursing elders, the child knew. When the elders fought and threw china cups at each other, the child knew. When the children threw tantrums and the grandmother thrashed them, the child knew. With the slightest commotion, the child knew it was time to withdraw. When the parents fought and blamed, it was time. When the grandmother began to see men with white beards gathering around her cot, it was time. When someone's glasses went missing or when the grandfather's rosary couldn't be found, it was time. When once in the month of June, the rains forgot to stop and the letters poured in just like water, it was time. It was time to withdraw to the backyard; time to reclaim her patch of land.

The letters became even more frequent than the visits of unexpected relatives. Someone in a public office, not far from Zébun's home, had decreed that Zébun's family did not belong to the land they had lived on for generations. Scores of letters in crisp envelopes barged into the house every other day. "Leave," the letters said. The lean postman stopped at the gate more often. The postman's bicycle grew accustomed to halting in front of the house, which was now beginning to resemble an old stooped man in his final years. The same envelopes arrived every time with similar stamps. The same looks were exchanged between the postman and any elder who received them. Letters coming in became as much a routine as Zébun sneaking out to the backyard. They were no different than the usual letters but the elders chose to call them 'notices' instead; elders with their strange ways and their habit of using different names for the same things. So a letter was called a notice. And more notices poured in. They became so frequent that they stopped bothering to open them. Perhaps because they contained the same content, the same few dry words written in a rough hand and sealed with wax in pale white envelopes. The postman visited so often that the house began to detest the very sight of his bicycle. The envelopes began to pile up. A new stack mounted next to the stack of old newspapers in the storeroom.

The stack continued to mount until the day a final letter arrived. A letter with the same words written in the same hand with the usual envelope and stamp. Only this time it wasn't just the letter. An hour after it was delivered, a group of men walked in through the gates. The visit stirred the house into action. Until that visit, the house had seemed what it had always seemed like: calm and safe. They weren't the old men in white clothes with white beards that only the grandmother had so often seen around her cot. They were tall young men, all in the same clothes, the clothes of a shade darker than the postman's uniform.

That morning, a storm raged outside and grew impatient for want of attention. But the house was too occupied to take notice. So the wind rattled the doors and shut the windows with loud thuds; the panes of some cracked. But the elders had no time. The dried slices of raw mangoes in the veranda remained unattended to. The dried chilies gathered dust. But the elders had no time. Old documents were vainly sought for. Moth-eaten papers were skimmed through. Pleas made. Pleas rejected. Appeals made, appeals denied. Eyes watered, eyes dried. Clothes tied in bundles, only to be untied again and the contents replaced with more important ones. Mattresses were rolled to resemble bales of hay. Kitchenware was fitted into large tin containers, only to be pushed closer to make space for a spoon here or a namakdaani there. The lids of baskets refused to close. In the storeroom, rusted trunks, probably as old as the grandmother herself, were brought down from the highest shelves. Grandmother's safes were unlocked. The old woman gathered her treasure in a bag sewn out of discarded bedsheets. Children's books had to be neglected. There were photo albums that needed space. Cobwebbed almirahs were opened. Lifeless documents were pinned together and pushed into suitcases. Letters in yellowing paper with missing envelopes were secretly tripped into pockets. Orders to make haste were heard. Take this, leave that; difficult choices made. More pleas made. More pleas rejected.

"Not your place," the visitors said. "Not your place," the children chanted. "Not your place," the house echoed. "Not your place," the child remembered.

And the child knew that it was time. She dragged a tiny wicker basket to the backyard and filled it with one, just one handful of soil from the kitchen garden. The house was vacated the same day; the city abandoned; the mosque loudspeaker never heard. And Zébun stopped eating mud. Whatever handfuls of it she had carried could not be eaten. The child refused any offers of it picked from the many roadside spots. The red soil of the mountains or the damp one on the riverbank, nothing pleased her. And not for once did the contents of the basket tempt her; it was as if the child had decided that it had to be saved, that it was the last of what she had taken away from the backyard, the last of what would remain of her childhood. The child knew. It was time. And so the elders walked. The grandmother lurched. The children ran. Baby Zébun, though no longer a baby but also not enough grown enough to be made to walk, was made to switch places. She went from one pair of adult shoulders to another. Elders taking turns. The child passed from arms with loose grips to warmer laps. Elders with moist eyes, children with confused faces, the grandmother with a burrowing hole in the heart. The child, expressionless. Only a basketful of soil, a handful of her land.

"THE EARTH SHALL TURN INTO PARADISE," "THERE'S STILL MUCH TO BE SAID," "IN THE ABSENCE OF MELODY," "THE RACE COMMENCES," AND "THE BOAT UNMOORS, O OARSMAN"

Avinash Chandra Vidyarthi, Awadhendra dev Narayan, and Aniruddh

Translated by Pitamber Kaushik

Translator's Note

Bhojpuri is native to and predominantly spoken in the Bhojpur-Purvanchal region of India (Bihar and eastern Uttar Pradesh) and the Terai region of Nepal. It also has sizeable bases of speakers in the countries of Fiji, Mauritius, Guyana, Suriname, and Trinidad and Tobago, among others. It is spoken by over 50 million people in India alone. Similar to Hindustani (Hindi-Urdu), it can be written in both the Devanagari script and the Nasta'liq (Urdu) script. The status of Bhojpuri as a language has been long debated, with some linguists considering it a distinct language and others opining it to be a sub-language or dialect of Hindi. Nonetheless, both native speakers as well as the diaspora and descendants of the native speakers consider Bhojpuri to be a crucial component of their respective cultural identities. There has been little effort to preserve Bhojpuri literature, partly owing to its lack of recognition as a distinct language in India as well as to the prejudice and stereotypes about the economically and educationally underdeveloped region which downplay its rich heritage. Due to a lack of historical and cultural awareness, translation efforts have been few and far between.

The five poems in this collection were chosen to reflect the diversity of Bhojpuri literature from psychosocial critique to motivational melodies, capturing everything from meditative natural rhythms to themes of urbanisation, migration, and social transformation. There is a pervasive stigma against the Bhojpuri language in contemporary India and a stereotype that compositions in Bhojpuri are crude, vulgar, lewd, garish, and kitschy. These prejudices have affected both the linguistic as well as the geocultural identities of Bhojpuri speakers, particularly in Bihar, a state with one of the lowest literacy rates, levels of industrialisation, and welfare-infrastructural development in India. Expressions of or through Bhojpuri language, literature, and culture are thus perceived as unscrupulous and uncouth in many parts of India, even Bihar itself. This curated collection of poems is aimed at helping to dispel such prejudice. These relatively lesser-known poems reflect a tradition rich in literary sophistication, keen observation, and philosophical wisdom. The three poets represented in this collection hail from different parts of Bihar, and the slight difference in the sub-dialects of Bhojpuri that they use is perceptible. They showcase the internal richness, diversity, and vibrance of the language through its subtly distinguished, finely nuanced variants. The poems are united in featuring a strong sense of community and unity in the highly diverse and largely agrarian state of Bihar. Humanism and social-knitting serve as unifying threads running through the works.

The poems are given below in the original script of Devanagari, then in transliteration using the IAST (International Alphabet of Sanskrit Transliteration) scheme, and finally, in English translation.

भुइँया सरग बनि जाई

अविनाश चन्द्र विद्यार्थी

आई, उहो दिन आई, अन्हरिया राति पराई
लीही अकासे छाई, किरिनि धरती पर धाई ।

कठमुरकी कन-कन के छूटी
सकदम साँस-साँस के टूटी
लीही पवन अँगडाई, गमक वन-वन छितराई ।

चह-चह बोल चुचूहिया बोली
जबदल कंठ मुरुगवा खोली
भँवरा पराती गाई, कली के मन मुसुकाई ।

डगर-डगर तब होई दल-फल
निसबद रही पाई ना जल-थल
जगरम घर-घर समाई, नगर में सोर सुनाई ।

भायी मोर, नयन ना निहँसी
धूमिल मुँह अँजोर में बिहँसी
भुइँया सरग बनि जाई, सुदिन तब साँच कहाई ।

BHUIṀYĀ SARAGA BANI JĀĪ

Avināśa Candra Vidyārthī

āī, uho dina āī, anhariyā rāti parāī
līhī akāse chāī, kirini dharatī para dhāī |

kaṭhamurakī kana-kana ke chūṭī
sakadama sāṁsa-sāṁsa ke ṭūṭī
līhī pavana aṁgaḍāī, gamaka vana-vana chitarāī |

caha-caha bola cucūhiyā bolī
jabadala kaṁṭha murugavā kholī
bhaṁvarā parātī gāī, kalī ke mana musukāī |

ḍagara-ḍagara taba hoī dala-phala
nisabada rahī pāī nā jala-thala
jagarama ghara-ghara samāī, nagara meṃ sora sunāī |

bhāyī mora, nayana nā nihaṁsī
dhūmila muṁha aṁjora meṃ bihaṁsī
bhūṁiyā saraga bani jāī, sudina taba sāṁca kahāī |

THE EARTH SHALL TURN INTO PARADISE

Avinash Chandra Vidyarthi

Indeed, even that day shall come to pass, when the dark night shall flee, it will;
Spreading over the sky, rays shall sprint on the Earth.

The indolence shall be lost from every grain,
The congestion of each breath shall rupture,
The breeze shall pandiculate, scattering fragrance throughout the woods.

The whistler bird shall chirrup in chuckles,
The rooster shall free its constricted throat,
The bumblebee shall drone the morning-carol, the heart of the bud shall beam.

Every trail shall then bloom and bustle,
No land or waters shall be able to stay wordless,
Awakening shall pervade every home, the commotion shall be heard in the town.

It shall please me, eyes shall never be downcast,
The ashen countenance shall twinkle in the light of dawn,
The Earth shall turn into Paradise, 'Good Times' shall then be deemed true.

Translator's Note:

1. Par āti is a genre of traditional devotional folk songs that often invoke certain deities and seek to awaken the household and
   neighbourhood. These auspicious melodies are sung at daybreak and traditionally draw from popular Hindu mythological
   narratives. Their recital is believed to rouse the listener's spirit and render the ambience propitious.

अबहीं बहुत कहे के बा

अविनाश चन्द्र विद्यार्थी

सुनि पवलीं हाँ अबहीं कहवाँ, अबहीं त बहुत कहे के बा।
गूँजत आइल बा राग जवन
मानीं, ह साँच बिहाग तवन
सुर सूतल जहाँ भैरवी के
उचरी तहवाँ अब काग कवन ?
खरकल ना एको पीपर पात, पवन उनचास बहे के बा।
रगवा पग के कठुआइल बा
ठगवा मग में हहुआइल बा,
गाँथी कइसे मोती लरिया
तगवा मन के अझुराइल बा
टुसिआई ठुँठी पाकड़िओ, कुछ दिन पतझार सहे के बा।
उड़ि के अइसन रहिया धइलीं
कलियन के संग भँवरा भइलीं
मधुआइल नयना भरमबलसि
माया का नगरी में अइलीं
निरभेद चदरिया तानीं जनि, सपना के महल ढहे के बा।
के आजु पराती गवले बा ?
जगरम के अलख जगवले बा ?
'धाव धाव'-कहि के केदो
अनदेखल के गोहरवले बा
जे जागत बा से पावत बा, बस लागल आतु के बा

ABAHĪṂ BAHUTA KAHE KE BĀ

Avināśa Candra Vidyārthī

suni pavalīṃ hāṃ abahīṃ kahavāṃ, abahīṃ ta bahuta kahe ke bā|

gūṃjata āila bā ah javana

mānīṃ, ha sāṃca bihāga tavana

sura sūtala jahāṃ bhaairavī ke

ucarī tahavāṃ aba kāga kavana ?

kharakala nā eko pīpara pāta, pavana unacāsa ah eke bā|

ragavā paga ke kaṭhuāila bā

ṭhagavā maga meṃ hahuāila bā,

gāṃthī kise motī lariyā

tagavā mana ke ajhurāila bā

ṭusiāī ṭhuṃṭhī pākaḍa○io, kucha dina patajhāra sahe ke bā|

uḍa○i ke aisana rahiyā dhilīṃ

kaliyana ke saṃga bhaṃvarā bhilīṃ

madhuāila nayanā bharamabalasi

māyā kā nagarī meṃ ailīṃ

nirabheda cadariyā tānīṃ jani, sapanā ke mahala ḍhahe ke bā|

ke āju parātī gavale bā ?

jagarama ke alakha jagavale bā ?

'dhāva dhāva'-kahi ke kedo

anadekhala ke goharavale bā

je jāgata bā se pāvata bā, basa lāgala ātu ke bā

THERE'S STILL MUCH TO BE SAID

Avinash Chandra Vidyarthi

Have I even had the chance to hear yet, there's still so much to be said,

The melody[1] that has drifted in reverberating,

Believe it! It's the true night-melody *Bihaag*;

Where the tune of the dawn-melody *Bhairavi* is itself asleep,

What crow would ever dare utter?

Not a leaf of the sacred fig rustled, myriad gusts are yet to blow.

The veins of my feet are petrified,

The thug[2] has turned impatient on the trail;

How do I thread a strand of pearls,

The strand of my mind is ravelled;

Tree-stumps are sprouting buds, a few days to bear the fall.

Taking the course of such a flight

That I turned into a bumblebee with the blossoms,

Mead-mellow eyes delirious with delusion,

I arrived in the city of illusions;

Their impregnable blankets are pulled over, the palace of dreams is bound to collapse.

Who chants the morning-carol these days?

Who awakens the zeal to awaken?

Who in the world urges, 'Hurry! Hurry!',

beckoning the unseen;

One who rises, receives, mere haste pervades!

Translator's Note:

1. 'Rāga' is a complex concept in Indian classical music systems, and it has no direct equivalent in Western music. It defines a broad melodic framework roughly resembling the concept of 'melodic modes'. Roughly, the 'Raga' is a specific yet spacious framework or musical aesthetic space within which a musical artist can improvise. It establishes the scope of a musical piece and provides the basic idea of the overall mood, spirit, and feel of the performance.
2. The word 'thug' historically referred to members of groups of highway and trunk-road bandits found in Northern India, who would ambush/deceive, strangle, and loot travellers, a practice called 'thuggee'. The word's meaning has significantly loosened in contemporary India and it is now used to refer to any swindler or fraudulent person, including petty conmen. Today, the word is frequently used as a mild pejorative.

बिनु गीत के

अविनाश चन्द्र विद्यार्थी

कुँहुँकत बा जहान बिनु गीत के
डहकत बा परान बिनु मीत के।

हरिअरिया बे-फुहार के झुरात बा
फुलवरिया ई बहार में धुँवाँत बा
धन्हकत बाटे आँचि अनरीत के।

बा लहरिया, ना नजरिया में हुलास बा
लहवरिया में नगरिया ई उदास बा
चहकत बा बिचार हार-जीत के।

मोहेला अल्हड़ करेज तनिक छोह से
सोहे ना बचनियाँ मुँह में मन का द्रोह से
सहकत बा सिंगार बे-पिरीत से।

झलकी रूप-रंग असली नवका भोर में
तनिका नेहिया लगवले जा अँजोर में
लहकत बाटे जियरा दियरा हीत के।
डहकत बा परान बिना मीत के॥

BINU GĪTA KE

Avināśa Candra Vidyārthī

kuṁhuṁkata bā jahāna binu gīta ke
ḍahakata bā parāna binu mīta ke|

hariariyā be-phuhāra ke jhurāta bā
phulavariyā ī bahāra meṁ dhuṁvāṁta bā
dhanhakata bāṭe āṁci anarīta ke|

bā lahariyā, nā najariyā meṁ hulāsa bā
lahavariyā meṁ nagariyā ī udāsa bā
cahakata bā bicāra hāra-jīta ke|

mohelā alhaḍa○ kareja tanika choha se
sohe nā bacaniyāṁ muṁha meṁ mana kā droha se
sahakata bā siṁgāra be-pirīta se|

jhalakī rūpa-raṁga asalī navakā bhora meṁ
tanikā nehiyā lagavale jā aṁjora meṁ
lahakata bāṭe jiyarā diyarā hīta ke|
ḍahakata bā parāna binā mīta ke||

IN THE ABSENCE OF MELODY

Avinash Chandra Vidyarthi

The world is snivelling in lack of melody,
The soul is whimpering in lack of its companion.

The greenery is shrivelling in want of showers,
The flower-yard is hazed in this spring,
The flame of disorder is flaring.

There is an uproar but no vigour in sight,
This city is gloomy in midst of festivities,
The deliberation of victory-and-loss is dinning.

The rambunctious heart is enchanted by the slightest trace of affection,
The words don't suit on the lips out of the dissent of the heart,
The Adornment is being unbridled lovelessly.

The true visage shall be glimpsed in the new dawn,
Adore me a little while the light (of the lamp) lasts,
The well-wisher's heart-lamp is burning;
The soul is whimpering for want of companionship.

दउर सुरू हो जाला

अवधेन्द्रदेव नारायण

सरेख मन से
गते-गते सँसरे में
करेज कसकेला।
बउराइल अकुलाहट
उफनात
जिंदिआ के
दउर लगावे में
इचिको ना थथमे।
फरीछ होते
जुड़ाइल
किरिन संगे चुप्पी सधले
सोना नियर दिन में
दउर सुरू हो जाला।
दूरी नापत
गहिर चाल से, धीरज बन्हले
नया बसेरा खोजत
जोत जगावत
दरद पी के
मन मुसक उठेला।
एही जिनगी के
निखरल खुलल दरपन बनेला
तबे नू
सरेख मन से।
गते-गते सँसरे में
करेज कसकेला।

DAURA SURŪ HO JĀLĀ

Avadhendradeva Nārāyaṇa

sarekha mana se

gate-gate saṁsare meṁ

kareja kasakelā|

baurāila akulāhaṭa

uphanāta

jidiā ke

daura lagāve meṁ

iciko nā thathame|

pharīcha hote

juḍaoāila

kirina saṁge cuppī sadhale

sonā niyara dina meṁ

daura surū ho jālā|

dūrī nāpata

gahira cāla se, dhīraja banhale

nayā baserā khojata

jota jagāvata

darada pī ke

mana musaka uṭhelā|

ehī jinagī ke

nikharala khulala darapana banelā

tabe nū

sarekha mana se|

gate-gate saṁsare meṁ

kareja kasakelā|

THE RACE COMMENCES

Awadhendra dev Narayan

Slow and steady,
gentle drifting
strains the heart.
The feverish fidgeting
doesn't relent in the least
in running the errands
of the foaming
frenzied fit.
With the crack of dawn
all gathered,
poised quietly with the raylets,
in the golden morrow,
the race commences.
Scaling the distance
with firm steps and intact composure
seeking a new dwelling
kindling a flame
gulping the ache
a smile radiates within
This itself becomes
life's refined, unobscured looking glass
Verily no wonder why,
slow and steady,
gentle drifting
strains the heart.

नाव खुले माँझी रे

अनिरूद्ध

पंछी चहके डेरात, कुनमुनात छवरा बा,
फुलवा महके डेरात, गुनगुनात भँवरा बा,
कुलबुलात भोर लुका, कुहरा के पहरा बा,
कुहा खुल माँझी रे, नाव खुल होसियार,
धार, लहर, जल, अकास, रँगवा चीन्हऽ बयार,
हइया रे हइया रे, भइया रे, थम्हले पतवार॥

चहचहा उड़े फर-फर, चिड़ई-मड़ई जागे,
गाय-भँइस खोल चले चरवाहा धुन रागे,
झटक चले बैला सँग, कान्हे हरवा-कुदार॥
चटक-मटक खिले कली, गमकल मग-गाँव-गली,
मतलब बहुते इयार, रसलोभी छली अली,
का सबेर दिलकली, खिले न जिया डर-अन्हार॥

प्यार धरम करम करे, हित जिनगी मेहनत बा,
बइठल मदवा स्वारथ, जियले में मउवत बा,
गैर कहाँ, के आपन, कुछ हमार ना तोहार॥
हाथ-हाथ जगरनाथ, हर देहिया खुदा एक,
एक रंग लहू हर तन, हर मजहब सदा एक,
हम सभ इनसान एक, भारत मइया हमार॥

पानी-दूधवा लजाय, भाई के खून पीअत,
धरम इहे मरदानी, अदमी ना अदमीअत,
बैरी के चाल मिलऽ, सुनलऽ भइया गोहार॥
साहस, बिसवास लगन, मिले कूल ठउआ ऊ,
जग सफर मुसाफिर हम, एक बा परउआ ऊ,
लगे जोर पहुँचा, पहुँचे नइया लगे पार॥
हइया रे हइया रे, भइया रे, थम्हले पतवार॥

NĀVA KHULE MĀṀJHĪ RE

Anirūddha

paṃchī cahake ḍerāta, kunamunāta chavarā bā,
phulavā mahake ḍerāta, gunagunāta bhaṁvarā bā,
kulabulāta bhora lukā, kuharā ke paharā bā,
kuhā khula māṁjhī re, nāva khula hosiyāra,
dhāra, lahara, jala, akāsa, raṁgavā cīnha' bayāra,
hiyā re hiyā re, bhiyā re, thamhale patavāra||

cahacahā uḍaoe phara-phara, ciḍaoī-maḍaoī jāge,
gāya-bhaṁisa khola cale caravāhā dhuna rāge,
jhaṭaka cale baailā saṁga, kānhe haravā-kudāra||
caṭaka-maṭaka khile kalī, gamakala maga-gāṁva-galī,
matalaba bahute iyāra, rasalobhī chalī alī,
kā sabera dilakalī, khile na jiyā ḍara-anhāra||

pyāra dharama karama kare, hita jinagī mehanata bā,
biṭhala madavā svāratha, jiyale meṃ mauvata bā,
gaaira kahāṁ, ke āpana, kucha hamāra nā tohāra||
hātha-hātha jagaranātha, hara dehiyā khudā eka,
eka raṃga lahū hara tana, hara majahaba sadā eka,
hama sabha inasāna eka, bhārata miyā hamāra||

pānī-dūdhavā lajāya, bhāī ke khūna pīata,
dharama ihe maradānī, adamī nā adamīata,
baairī ke cāla mila', sunala' bhiyā gohāra||
sāhasa, bisavāsa lagana, mile kūla ṭhauā ū,
jaga saphara musāphira hama, eka bā parauā ū,
lage jora pahuṁcā, pahuṁce niyā lage pāra||
hiyā re hiyā re, bhiyā re, thamhale patavāra||

THE BOAT UNMOORS, O OARSMAN

Aniruddh

The bird is afraid of chirping, the kid is afraid of stirring,

The blossom fears divulging a whiff, the bumblebee is humming,

The mist stands guard over the tucked restless dawn;

Heed, O Oarsman!, Part the fog, part with the dock, O wise one!

The currents, the waves, the water, and the sky, do discern the complexion of the breeze,

Ahoy, Heave—Ho! Heave-Ho!, holding on to the oar.

Taking flight, fluttering away with a trill, the birds have arisen along with the field-huts,

The herder has untethered the cattle, crooning a rapturous strain,

The tiller has set off for the fields, oxen at his side, shoulder laden with plough, spade, and hoe.

Here and there brilliant blossoms blooming, every road, town, and street infused with fragrance,

Myriad, believe it, thirsting deceptive bumblebees,

What love-bud would blossom, the self fears unfurling in the dark.

Love, Integrity, and Duty, a life of favour is one of labour

Staying put with ego, a life of self-service is lifeless.

Where's a stranger to be found? Who's your own? None of mine, none of yours.

Every hand, the world's master, in every embodiment of self, the Almighty,

The same shade of red fills every body, every faith ever one,

We are one, the land our mother.

Milk and water look on abashed, as the blood of brethren quenches thirst.

This, verily the hero's code, human sans humanity.

Towards the steps of the ill-wisher, heed my imploration!

Courage, Faith, and Diligence, the bank shall be gotten to.

The world a voyage, we the voyagers, united in destination

Harder! spare no effort, have the boat reach ashore

Ahoy, Heave—Ho! Heave-Ho!, holding on to the oar.

DREAMLAPSE

Monica Kim

CW: Sexual Assault

When you dream, how do you know you're in your own body? Does your mind take you down paths you don't recognize, does it create shadowy figures in the periphery of your vision, does it hurt when you jerk awake and hit your head against the slanted ceiling of your bedroom?

What I mean to say is, do you remember your dreams; do you inhabit your dreams; do you become your dreams; do your dreams represent someone else from the past?

The diary is falling apart. If I don't tie it together with a rubber band, it'll separate, the cover and pages coming cleanly off the spine.

I open to the middle of a random page and bring my face against the paper, breathing as if I could absorb the words with my nose—it's musty, and there's something faint there, that old paper smell.

When I look at the page, at twelve-year-old me's handwriting, the lead slightly smudged against lined paper, I want to bring her back—not that I want to be her again—but it feels like there should be a recognition in my writing, in these pages, in my memories. Yet all I am is in the dark, empty room of my childhood, in the house of my upbringing, the place my parents are finally abandoning.

I flip to the next page. *Today I dreamt . . .*

<u>May 7 2010</u>

- *fabric? blanket? under me*
- *5? 10? 15? men w/ same haircut*
    - *they looked like . . . maybe military?*
    - *i dont remember*
- *dr. moon said it was ok if i couldnt remember everything + it was nice of him to say that but i dont rlly like him*
- *sometimes i think he stands too close to me*

Dr. Moon. I remember him. I only went into his office for a few months, after convincing my mom that I wasn't having any more dreams (a lie) and that anyways, his treatments weren't working (a truth).

- *all the men wear the same clothes*
- *1 woman*
    - *shes lying next to me? (but "me" isnt actually "me." idk how old "me" in my dream is but her body is skinnier than me + she has longer hair + shes kind of dirty like she hasnt taken a shower in days. idk her name but her name isnt mine. idk . . .)*

Even reading this, ten years later, with what I know now, it's still confusing to me. How could I have been dreaming of someone, inhabiting someone's body, who wasn't me, but who was real? Whose name I didn't know, still don't know, but *has* to be real?

In my last year of undergrad, we read *Make It Scream, Make It Burn* by Leslie Jamison and even though I'd skimmed most of the book—not because I didn't like it, but because I had a million other readings for other classes plus graduation plus the stressful uncertainty of my future plus juggling a job—one chapter stuck out to me, still sticks out to me now, and that was the only chapter I read with such detail and care that I underlined almost every sentence.

The story comes back to me now: in "We Tell Ourselves Stories in Order to Live Again," there was a boy named James who has dreams from the memories of a World War II soldier. He knows his name, his fellow soldiers' names, even the plane the soldier flew in. How could a teenager know such details so specifically, without ever having read about the soldier before? James never wanted to be a soldier, had never been interested in World War II before these dreams.

I never learned about the Japanese atrocities against Korean women in World War II until college. And I would never, ever want to inhabit the body of the girl in my dreams.

- *red mark on left side of her face*
- *feels like red mark on my (but not <u>my</u>) face*

I flip the diary pages to a few months back. My fingers twitch, and I resist the urge to read in a linear fashion. After all, aren't dreams and memories cyclical?

<u>**Feb 2 2010**</u>

- *its weird starting my diary again, but only for my dreams*
- *i stopped writing when i started 6th gr last yr since no one would think im cool but dr. moon (new dr. – mom + dad finally decided to take me since i was still having those weird dreams even after they sprayed holy water on my pillow. not that i rlly believed that would work . . .) said it might help to write my dreams down*
- *ok my dream . . . no one is gonna find these one day + read them, right?*

No one except twelve-year-old me and current, twenty-two-year-old me.

- *only thing i remember from last night (early this morning?) were hands*
    - *dont think they were my (the girl's) hands bc they were bigger + they had lots of calluses*
- *dream shifted to woman giving birth to baby, baby that wasnt me (the girl)*

So much of it is coming back to me now. Dreams of a policeman telling me—the girl whose body I was in—about work in a factory in Japan, how so many girls like me left Korea for good, honest work, to help our struggling families. Dreams of my mother and father and my baby brother lying together on the floor, huddled for warmth as the wind whipped outside. Whispers between my parents about what they should do; silent arguments and agreements about what I could do. Dreams of me hugging my family goodbye, resolutely dry-eyed as I left home, found the policeman, who transferred me and other girls my age and younger and older—but not much older—to Japanese soldiers, who looked at us in a way that made my skin crawl, who looked at us, my heart immediately dropping, wondering if, after all, those rumors had been true. Dreams of dark spaces, dreams of being blindfolded, dreams of not knowing where I was, dreams of waking up in a room with five other women, our bodies immobile, our cries silent. Dreams of a rough hand grabbing my wrist, of multiple men surrounding me, all Japanese soldiers, of passing out and waking up with a terrible pain in between my legs. Dreams of combing another woman's hair, of tending to the bruises and cut lips and internal injuries no one could see, of removing the crab lice from my friend's pubic hair. Dreams of writing a letter to my father and mother and baby brother, no longer a baby, a letter none of them would receive. Dreams of the letter burning and the fire colliding with my skin. Dreams of winters where the snow reached my knees. Dreams of summers where sweat stuck to every crevice of my body. All in this unbearable little room. Dreams of soldiers leaving, of whispers about the war ending, of the little blossom of hope opening inside me.

<u>Oct 29 2010</u>

- *ik im supposed to be writing abt my dreams but im so angry abt what happened @ school today i have to write abt this instead*
- *we were learning abt sex (ew) + i asked a few qs bc i wanted to know if this is what was happening in my dreams but chris kept making fun of me + laughing + asked if i rlly wanted to do it so much, why didnt i just ask any boy in the room, except oh, no one would want me because im chinese*

The first time I met Chris, we had been assigned seats next to each other in homeroom. On the first day of sixth grade, when I sat down next to him, he turned toward me. When he opened his mouth, I thought he might say hello, but instead he said, loud enough for the rest of the class to hear, "Chinese commie!" and pointed finger guns at me, *pew pew*.

I glared at him. "I'm Korean."

He stared at me, then pulled out the finger guns again. "North Korean commie!" *Pew pew.*

I remember digging my fingernails so deeply into the palms of my hands, wanting to punch him so bad, knowing I'd get in trouble if I did. I was so angry that no one bothered to distinguish between Chinese and Korean, and yet today I'm sitting with the fact that although the Japanese military sexually enslaved Korean women and girls, they had also raped and sexually enslaved women and girls from China, Taiwan, the Philippines, Indonesia, East Timor, the Netherlands, Malaysia . . .

In the end, you were just another body to wreak violence unto.

- *i told him for the millionth time that im korean + i didnt want to do 'it' w/ anyone + just leave me the fuck alone then everyone made a big deal of me saying fuck + ms. friedman (**<u>FUCK HER</u>**) pulled me aside to give me a warning then apologize to chris + that i shouldnt ask "inappropriate questions"*
- *ugggghhhh. he can go rot in hell*
- *felt like crying before but now im just angry. i **<u>HATE</u>** this school.*

I hated school then, feeling so out of place, being one of the only few Asians in my middle-school and high-school years. And yet—it was through school that I first learned about those women, in my college years. Through school I took an international feminism class, through school I learned about the survivors who protested outside of the Japanese embassy in Seoul every Wednesday, through school I learned about the kid who had strange dreams like mine.

<u>*June 14 2011*</u>

- *1st time i havent had dream in over 1 yr. **<u>THE !!! FIRST !!! TIME !!!</u>***
- *no soldiers. no girls*
    - *no blankets no bruises no guns no small room no letters*
- *N O T H I N G*
- *feels so good to dream of nothing*

I close the diary, leaning back against the wall of my old bedroom. I close my eyes.

Coincidentally (although I'm beginning to think not so coincidentally) this last diary entry was from my first trip to South Korea. My parents and I flew to Daegu, to visit my grandfather's new burial site.

The Korean summer hadn't become too unbearably humid yet, but I felt hyper-aware of strangers' eyes on me, lingering over my shorts and tank top. Mom gave me a sweater to cover my shoulders, but the fabric felt too itchy against my skin. People could stare at me all they wanted under the cover of their umbrellas, hiding themselves from the strength of the sun.

When we reached my grandfather's burial site, my parents knelt on their knees and murmured prayers in Korean, making a sign of the cross over themselves and over the framed photograph of my grandfather. They offered a pear, dried fish, and jeon for his soul.

I hate to admit it, but I zoned out while they were doing this. My grandfather passed away when I was two years old; I had barely any memory of him. The only way I knew him was through photographs and my dad's very few anecdotes. My mind wandered, and my eyes fell over the other burial sites, the other families kneeling and praying next to us.

How many of these people had been alive during the Korean War, during Japanese colonization? How many had felt a gun to the back of their heads, pressed there by American soldiers who mistook them for communists? How many women laid here, and were any of these women the women like the girl I inhabited in my dreams?

A shudder came over me, and I felt a tightness in my chest, something that stretched deep into the very ends of my bones. All of a sudden, I felt like I wanted to cry—to let out a wail, to pound my fists against the grass and to curl into a fetal position. My grandfather had been alive during Japanese colonization, during World War II, during the Korean War—he had survived it all. But did he have any sisters? Mothers? Aunts? Were any of them taken away? Did he and his family have to cross over the newly made, arbitrarily drawn border, to the same land that was now called a different country? Did he have to leave any of his family behind—grandparents, small children, disabled siblings—because they were seen as weak, because they thought they wouldn't be able to make it? Who did he lose?

"Mi-Young." Out of nowhere, my mother's voice came to me. She motioned for me to kneel, to join her and my father in prayer.

I did as I was told, my knees feeling warm against the summer ground. I didn't have the words for prayer, at least not for my grandfather. But I pictured the young girl of my dreams. In that moment, I called her Jae-Young, after my grandmother's sister, who died during the war.

Jae-Young. Did you ever make it home? When you closed your eyes, were you able to see the mountains and rolling hills of your homeland? I don't know if you ever made it back. But I am here. I am home.

I tuck the journal underneath my arm, bound down the stairs, past the living room that is empty save for a few boxes, out the door, and sit on the front steps, breathing in the summer rain. My parents are coming to gather the rest of the boxes soon—I had asked them for some time alone to say goodbye to this childhood home. The young girl I dreamt of—the young girl I named Jae-Young, briefly, in Daegu—comes back to me. Dragon eyes, middle-parted, coarse, black hair, rounded cheeks.

I can't say for certain if my return to South Korea all those years ago meant Jae-Young's homecoming, too, and if the return of her soul to her homeland meant her soul leaving my dreams, leaving my subconscious. The timing seems too coincidental, and yet—I remember that boy, James, was only able to stop dreaming from the soldier's body after he and his parents went to Japan and set out on a boat in the middle of the Pacific Ocean, bursting into tears, holding each other as the boat rocked amidst the waves.

"Jae-Young," I whisper out loud, and then I clear my throat, open my mouth wider. "Jae-Young." I don't know if that is your actual name; it feels wrong to misname you, but it feels even more wrong to not give you a name at all.

"Jae-Young." Louder. Louder. Louder, still, and then I'm running back into the house, returning to the spot in the living room where we did jesa, where we honored my male ancestors on my father's side. I never understood why we only offered food to the men in my father's line, and never the women or the ancestors on my mother's side. When I asked my parents about this once, they mumbled something about tradition or culture.

Perhaps what I'm about to do is sacrilege. But my hands move of their own accord, placing the diary in the middle of the dusty floor, as if it were a table replete with a feast.

I bring my hands in front of me and bow to my knees, my forehead kissing the dusty wooden floorboard. I bow, again. I stand, and I bow, my back perpendicular to the floor. An offering.

"Jae-Young," I say, out loud, my voice echoing in the room full of ghosts of the past. I cough, clearing my throat again. It feels awkward to do this, but I can't stop. I say the names of some of the halmeoni we know:

Kim Hak-Sun

Yun Tu-Ri

Kim Kayako

Pak Ok-Nyon

Kim Young-Im

Mun P'il-Gi

Hwang Kum-Ju

Lee Ok-Seon

Gil Won-Ok

Pak Ok-Sun

Kang Soon-Shim

Lee Young-Ok

Kim Eun-Rye

Kim Gun-Ja

Mun Ok-Ju

Lee Ji-Sook

Kim Bok-Dong

Kim Han-Soon

Kang Duk-Kyung

Lee Yong-Su

The list is incomplete.

I stand up straight again, moving my body side to side. I brush the dust off my knees, grab the diary, look around the living room once more, and before my parents can find me here and wonder what I'm doing standing alone in this haunted room, I leave for my spot on the front door steps again.

Jae-Young, it feels wrong to not give you a face, a story. There are so many women, halmeoni, like you, who have not been able to return home. Some may have received money but no one's received an apology, recognition from the Japanese government. Not even a court in South Korea pins the violence onto Japan. Not even some historians in America recognize this violence.

Something blooms in my chest, the same emotion I'd felt all those years ago in Daegu.

Han.

There are more of you dying. Only a few are left, to impart your memories and experiences to us, to remember the pain that wreaked havoc against your bodies and your minds and your souls. It feels like time is slipping away from us, that your wrinkled hands and crooked teeth and moles scattered across your bodies like constellations are moving farther and farther away from us, one foot slowly inching towards the other side. When you leave, I hope we don't forget you. When you leave, I hope this never happens again.

One day, I hope you'll find peace.[1]

---

[1] Learn more about the women sexually enslaved by the Japanese military during World War II, euphemistically called "comfort women": https://comfortwomenaction.carrd.co/

SAMIRA

Atar Hadari

I tell you something, when the sun shining, nothing can hurt you. When you see someone, you know what they good for. You see in their face, like I see in your face, I see you kind. Some people, I go up and down, up and down the streets in the German Colony, all the way along Bethlehem Road, sometimes in the shade, sometimes not, I go all the way to their house, not a cup of water, nothing, not today, some people—you, always a kind word. How's your wife? I saw her the other day, down by the mall. She doesn't look so good. She doing ok? You need any jobs done, need a little help round here? You help Samira, I help you every day. I come from my village, I help you, every day, I don't mind the journey.

You and me, we're like one family. You know my son, with the leg? He's not very well. I come, I don't mind, every day, the check point doesn't bother me—I was born here, they can't stop me coming. I come every day to get food for my family. But when his leg needs a new hip, that I can't get on Bethlehem Road. That I need some help. You know your wife? I told her about my son, when I saw her. She said you'd help. She said she was sorry. What good is sorry, I tell her, it comes from Allah, you want to be sorry? A little help for someone in your family, then you don't have to be sorry for anything. You been living here long? You look like you belong here. You grow anything in this garden? Back in my village, this much land, you could feed all your children. You only have that one? Inshallah, next year, you'll have another one. Then you can plant this garden with what—carrots, onions, turnips? You feed them, all strong sons. You need any help with your garden?

My son? Thanks for asking. Not good. The hip, the hip all rotten. Fifteen and he needs a hip. Is that funny? I'm an old woman, my hip's like iron, he's a boy barely shaves, his hip snaps like a twig. Allah. He knows what he's doing. But I have to find the medicine. Money. You sure you know what you're doing with this garden? You want a little help? Ok. Sure, sure. Thursday. I bring my brother and husband's brother. They help. They very good potato planters. The best. They make this patch of grass an oasis. You'll look out of your window you won't know where you live, so many onions coming from the ground. You won't be able to walk to the gate, you'll have to fight so many leaves. Ok. Till Thursday. Give my love to your wife. She looks like she needs a little something.

You know my son? His leg is worse. I say his leg, really his hip but he tried to walk, stupid boy, to get me a glass of milk. Since he was so high he been trying take care of me. Isn't that stupid? He's too stupid to stay off his hip which is rotten, so now he broke the shin as well, where he fell down into the rock-hard garden we got 'cause we can't get any water, not like here. What's that? You got trouble with water. Everybody got trouble with water. Your wife? What's the matter with your wife? I saw her again the other day, circles under her eyes and she looked as white as that glass of milk my son spilled . . . she got frightened? What's there to be frightened about water? Zionists? Eh, I don't mean to be anything but, Mister, you have a kipah on your head and a beard—it's not so long but it's there. I think my brother and my husband there, they probably think you're a Zionist too. Your wife she's scared of Zionists? How you get that kid you playing with? Ah, not you. She got other Zionists. You got Zionists knocking on you door, too? How come? This is Jerusalem, and you wife and you look—well—you look pretty close to Ben Gurion to me—how come you got? You had people in your yard. Ah, neighbours. Tsk. I know about neighbours. Thing about neighbours is, you can't shoot them because they can always shoot back. I'm just kidding, honestly.

I'm not political. So what did your neighbours do? Friends of your neighbour—what did they do? They came by and watered your garden. Hmm. I don't get it. They washed your windows? No. They splashed on your patio? No. I give up. What did they do your wife didn't like? She's scared of Zionists? Well, I don't know to tell you, me, sometimes, Samira gets a little scared too. But if they wanted to come water my garden, you know what I'd say, Begin and Ariel Sharon they can come too. They want to water Samira's garden, I give them tea, a little sumsum, maybe cake.

She hid under the bed? That's not good. Your wife hid under the bed when the Zionists came? Does she like it here? I not sure if I like Israel, you know, I love Jerusalem but I don't love every check point, but I never hid under my bed when the IDF go by. She hide under the bed when the neighbour friend come water your garden, I think you need help from more than Samira. I think maybe she want more than onion growing in this ground. She pregnant again? Praise Allah. I'm sure she look into that baby face, she see a big fat Zionist can chase off all the neighbours and get back all your water rights. No Zionist going to push your baby around, he going to be big and strong and kick them back where they belong. Right? So where you want us to start with digging this ground?

My son's leg? Ahmed—how many stitches in Hassan's leg? Forty-seven? You tell lies like an elephant. How I got married to that man I don't know. I loved his lies and then I had a wedding and a son before I was seventeen. But no—it wasn't forty-seven or thirty-seven. Maybe twenty stitches. We got a nurse in the village can do stitches. The hip is what I need to dig your garden for. Don't be silly, I'm not expecting to take all your money. You see my teeth? All rotten, like my son's hip, but one or two is made of gold. So. Like that. I just want one or two teeth made out of gold, to dig out of your ground. The rest can be rotten teeth. I'm used to eating with them. I bite hard no matter what my tooth is made of. I can bite into metal since I'm little. I don't feel anything anymore. You want your onions here? Or I got carrots. These, very special carrots. Not like what you buy in the supermarket. Are you kidding me? You joking with Samira. You think you could go to your supermarket and buy carrots and just put them in the ground and wow they come up. You have a little bit to learn about this garden, even if you do belong here. You don't get anything from just a little sweat. You find the right place, you find the right kind of carrot, you make the right hole, you put the water in the right way. You trust Samira. My brother and my husband they start digging now, right now, right after they eat. And you see. You see if you can walk out of this gate, before the new year. I make a deal with you. You walk out of this gate by new year and I'll give you back my poor son's hip. You can have it instead. It can make your salad bitter, instead of the onion. Just joking. I know you wouldn't eat onion with your salad. You look like you like things sweet.

What about flowers here? You don't got room for flowers? What about your son—your son doesn't want to pull up things? You don't give him flowers to pull up, he'll pull up onions. He's a Zionist, isn't he? Give him flowers to look at or he'll take away you land. Zionists love to water things so they look like Poland, I heard all about it on Channel 1. You want they start to dig? They finished their hummus. Thank you very much for the water in the cups. Really. You wouldn't imagine how many people we go work for never offer you a cup touched their lips. I won't come in. I stay out here with my husband and brother. You go in, get your little Zionist under the shade. He's only little. Let him crawl a little, while he has the use of his leg.

That's it. We come back tomorrow, water the plantings, put a few more things into the holes. Over there, you got onions. Over there, potatoes. Over there, carrots. No flowers, not an inch that's flowers. You can trust me on that. You won't have poppies come up like the Wizard of Oz? You see that movie? We see that movie all the time in Palestine. When she clicks her heels together and says, "There's no place like home"—every little boy and girl in Ramallah says, "No place like home". I don't believe in the flying monkeys. I think that some silly Jew wrote that in America. But the cowardly lion, and the witch, and the scarecrow—we all believe in scarecrows who haven't got any brains. How's your wife doing? She crawled out from under the bed yet? What you mean she had another scare? Yeah I know it was Independence Day yesterday. We call it Nakba, but it's more or less a direct translation. You don't celebrate? Sure we celebrate. Oh yeah, now you mention it, I guess there are celebrations in this street. Who marched up here? The Bnei Akiva—who they?—the little Zionists? What they do, fire water pistols? Oh, wave flags. That's nice. Who else marched? The Palestinian youth? Ah, that's funny. What did they do—throw potatoes? I'm joking. You got us planting potatoes, what you need the little Palestinians for—what they do, really? They marched and waved flags. Ok—what's your wife's problem? She under the bed again? Oh—she couldn't tell the difference. You tell her—the Palestinian kids were the ones singing in Arabic and looking over their shoulders. She wants, I'll come over next Nakba and point them out to her. We can eat the onions, sitting together in the shade. I see you tomorrow, we all come finish to plant.

How you doing today? My son's hip better, thank you. Well, the bone starting to knit. We see how he walks when the cast it come off but, thank Allah, I got the hip, he got the doctor. I was born here, you know, I told you. But my husband, my husband, like my son, was born in Bethlehem, so they get no free doctor. They pay. That's why he dig your land. What you mean you want no more? Your wife doesn't want the vegetables? She crawled under the bed again—I come inside and help you drag her out. She not under the bed? She gone to your neighbour. What neighbour? Oh, friend. A woman friend or man friend? Oh, woman friend—then she could still come back. Where your boy? You let her take him? What kind of Zionist are you? I didn't think Zionists were like that. Soft. You tell her this. She should come back to this garden. She don't want me to water it, I won't water it. She don't think Samira is Zionist eh? She not that far gone. You tell her, I don't march here next Nakba and nobody else march here next Nakba. I sit with her and we eat onions together. Tell her I want her to come back and meet my son. I want your son to chase my son. By the time he walking, my son be walking again. And we all sit here and eat onion together. You like onion? I want her to eat onion with my son because marching don't get you your garden back. Just a little onion here, a little onion there. You plant enough onions before you know it every Zionist know your name and maybe, just maybe, when you get into an argument with him about the water—nobody start shooting. Just a little argument. Between neighbours. You like that uh? You tell her the Zionist is in her belly and she got to come back here, just like I had to go there. I had to go there because I had my husband's baby in between my rib cage and no matter how much I wanted to be in Jerusalem, I knew where I belong. And she now belong here. You tell her that. And you come back and we eat onion together. I want her to eat onion with my son. You tell her that, ok? I want her to sit and eat onion with me on Nakba day and we go look together at the boys go marching with their flags and we spray them with water. You do that for me, say that to her? I won't let anybody chase her under the bed. I be a friend to her. You tell her that. I think she need a friend to save her from the Zionists. Tell her, if I can live with them, maybe she can too. I be her family. I told you, we all family. You go tell her and I plant one more thing for you. A flower. Right here. You tell her to come back and watch it grow, so she can be here when her son comes to tear it out.

WINNERS OF THE 8ᵀᴴ SINGAPORE POETRY CONTEST

We're very pleased to announce the results of the 8th annual Singapore Poetry Contest. In conjunction with our Gaudy Boy launch of Jhani Randhawa's prizewinning book of poems *Time Regime*, this year's contest looked for poems that used the chiming words "time" and "regime" together or separately in imaginative ways. Poems should also possess overall excellence, of course. Open to everyone, the contest was judged by our Editor-in-Chief Jee Leong Koh. Winners receive a cash prize and publication in SUSPECT.

We received a total of 245 poems. The entries came from 27 countries from around the world. Singapore leads with 67 entries, followed by the US 35 (CA 11, NY 4, PA 4, NC 3, VA 3, MN 2, NV 2, MA 1, MD 1, MO 1, SC1, TN 1, TX 1), Nigeria 31, India 19, the UK 9, the Philippines 8, South Africa 8, Benin 7, Canada 6, Uganda 5, Malaysia 4, Pakistan 4, Austria 3, Ecuador 3, Australia 2, Bolivia 1, Congo 1, Germany 1, Ghana 1, Hong Kong 1, Indonesia 1, Israel 1, Italy 1, New Zealand 1, Spain 1, Ukraine 1, Zimbabwe 1, and 23 entries from unknown locations.

First Prize

THE FUNERAL DIRECTOR SAID H/IS/ER BODY DIDN'T CHECK

Gabriel Awuah Mainoo

imagine at midnight Jesus comes down from the cross to eat pomegranates// imagine the dead is dug again & again & again// & examined if their genitals could make an ovum out of the clammy bog// of course everyone witnesses it on TV & radio & placards in newspapers & magazines// the protest for unitary bathrooms// at the last LGBT-gathering s/he said the next country s/he'd love to visit is located in-between that Mexican wo/man's thighs// i asked h/im/er about allegiance// s/he lithographed a garnet smile in my stomach// a galaxy of invisible azaleas rearranging on my hedged-lid// s/he confessed s/he's left a part of h/er/him with every man & every wo/man forgets their part in h/im/er// pulling coffee out of everyone's body makes me understand thermodynamics// it's not the science// such sci-miracle occur when the knee of a black-muscular-wo/man & a white-feminine-man// a white-muscular-wo/man & a black-feminine-man// a black-muscular-wo/man & a black-feminine-man// a white-feminine-man & a white-muscular-wo/man is deep in another// even the thing doesn't have a name// conjure it out of nomenclature like Sadi Carnot// the name is not a thing// calling it a thing isn't enough// enough// to you is acceptance// but acceptance is what you don't want to accept// or acceptance is not enough?// sexuality is a toothed-wind loitering beyond every regime of time// i don't know// i don't know// i don't know how that chimney sweeper knows everyone's favorite sex position in that office// it's the thing nobody wants to accept// probably s/he is addicted to the lethal smoke in everyone's breath// what is not there is what you are not seeing// from the tail of the supreme court i see the KFC truck turning at point X// in the disappearance two women kissing in the fog of chicken smell beside the old grand cathedral overlooking the police station// arriving at locus Y// is a brothel named after a bleeding government// i see warm hands of gay boys climbing & lowering on bodies behind the cloud-pile of Cedar-wood// what is there is what you are not seeing// the confusion & neglect flings us here// to excavate the gender of this poem// gunshots of voices// incendiary placards & armed words minced into armors & cudgels// how many times do you want to bury the dead? mulberry skin// the complexion of hundred countries// today you are the size of rain in the clouds// i only identify you// after you gather in my hands// tenderly, i throw you back into the skies// survive//

Judge's Comment:

What impresses me about "The funeral director said h/is/er body didn't check" is the largeness of the world it encompasses. I'm thinking not only of the external reality of "two women kissing in the fog of chicken smell beside the old grand cathedral overlooking the police station" but also of the interior space opened up by "a galaxy of invisible azaleas rearranging on my hedged-lid." I'm thinking of Jesus Christ's Jerusalem, William Blake's London, and Sadi Carnot's Paris—religion, politics, and science. Despite, or is it because of, the forward slashes of separation, what knits the disparate spaces and references together is the poetic voice, at once wondering, skeptical, amused, and tender. I will not forget the memorable image that the poem makes of the contest's challenge: "sexuality is a toothed-wind loitering beyond every regime of time," with its ineffable mixture of longing, pain, hope, and, perhaps, political resistance.

Second Prize

UNTITLED

Purbasha Roy

Much later from today, all that's between us
shall breathe *timeproof*. Tell me, if something
never loses value what word graces it better
meaning than *timeless*. I have explored the
regime of this feeling and found it has margins
made of dawn things. A whole cosmos blooming
within, *timed-out* from sorrows; nightmares. The
sunshafts falling cursive around us. Like *timeous*
ballads of consolations we finally stumbled as sky
wearing its own body. At nucleus of our bruises,
now taking *regimented* journey of collapsing. Inside
their own *time-lapsed* histories. You say, the shores
of our shadows shall seek each other like *timeliest*
train-boarding from a village station where trains
arrive once a week. Let me admit I want to adjust
this *time* to that type of *time* which on condensing
kneels soundlessly towards the farceless door of home

Judge's Comment:
I love this poem for its cheeky wit. It takes up the contest challenge and plays it like a hand-held xylophone. The musicality of
the wit here is accompanied by the gorgeousness of the imagery ("nucleus of our bruises"), which aptly simplifies towards the
village station, towards home at the end. Love poems are hard to write. The imagination sparked here speaks convincingly of
love's fire.

Third Prize

IF NOT A DEAD NOUN VERB-ING TOWARDS A DEADER NOUN

Chisom Charles Nnanna

I've ceased wondering what will happen to the universe
if I exit this body suddenly. I've seen powerful men

become nothing more than morphemes in my
history textbook.

Is time and emptiness not the same traveller?

It happens I've been living another's universe.
I walk to my reflection and it's not facing me; it's walking

to another's reflection.
This body I'm in is a rudder swayed by someone else, something else.

I'm still remembering when all that could go right went
depressingly wrong when I called my own shots.

Charles, really, did they?

What is it about making a mark that makes us go as
far as ~~conveniently~~ un-gathering ourselves and

knitting masks to our skin?

What is a Republic without her own regime if not a
dead noun verb-ing towards a deader noun?

I pray I do not fall into that timeless sleep living a
poem like this.

I want to own	this universe
this reflection	this ship
this country	this body.

Judge's Comment:

This poem successfully evokes the uncanny feeling of living in someone else's universe, in someone else's body. Our reflection, what we take for granted, may walk away from us. Our agency, what we value so highly, may do us in. This has always been the case, the poem admonishes itself, in the history of great men and in the current moment of the Republic. We can only pray and state plainly what we want.

IN PRAISE OF RADICAL SLOWNESS

Review of How I Became a Tree *(India: Aleph Books, 2017) and* VIP: Very Important Plant *(London: Shearsman, 2022) by Sumana Roy*

Reviewed by Shalini Sengupta

Sumana Roy's emerging oeuvre bears testimony to the richness and variety of Indian women's writing in English. Roy leans into what is life-giving while simultaneously confronting the consumptive, nihilistic death cults—capital, speed, servitude, mortgage, wage labour—that seek to divide and manage human beings. Her writing is rich in specificity and steeped in the particularities of the communities it seeks to describe. Her *How I Became a Tree* and *VIP* appear as odes to all that is neglected: books that capture the significance of plants as well as the legacies of colonial violence and displacement that can be understood through a focus on plants. Taken together, they allow a glimpse into Roy's trailblazing new work on plant humanities, which is prompted by the desire to reposition eco-critical literature from below and render it more open to the experiences of the marginalised other.

How I Became a Tree begins on a note of disaffection: "I was tired of speed. I wanted to live to tree time". In her praise of critical slowness, which is achieved through the phrase "tree time", Roy appears nuanced and provocative. She offers searing critiques of discipline, of disciplinary power in a broad historical and sociopolitical sense and in academic and artistic circles. Roy writes, "my amorphous fancies about trees began to coalesce when I entered middle age and began to weigh the benefits of a freelancer's life against that of a salaried professional". She continues, "when I look back at the reasons for my disaffection with being human, and my desire to become a tree, I can see that at root lay the feeling that I was being bulldozed by time". "Tree time" allows the poet-narrator to experience the world inverted, presented with new value beyond utilitarian contexts. It opens a space of possibility that enables another vision of how our lives might proceed. Roy's language is descriptive and located. Her writing offers a jolt of reorientation, a palpable reminder of an all-but-vanished way of living and a hitherto unexpected world.

The book proceeds by unraveling expectations of people, art, and ecologies. It is at once forceful and tender, highlighting the vulnerability of the heart even as it explodes the hierarchies of this "deadlined world". Roy's narrative is as poignant and deeply personal as it is overtly political. Early sections of the book, such as "Women as Flowers", unpick the diminutive qualities that are ascribed to women and flowers alike. Later sections span various genres. They appear steeped in myth and memory, Bangla folktales and fairy lores that have traversed generations. There's a sharp delight in the manner in which she curates a distinctly South Asian—or, rather, Indian—archive, one informed by the writing of artists and thinkers who have thought about plant-human interactions intellectually, emotionally, and intuitively. Here, Roy casts her net wide. She alludes to the work of Indian writers of children's fiction, such as Dakshinaranjan Mitra Majumdar; Indian poets such as Rabindranath Tagore and Shakti Chattopadhyay; Indian novelists such as Balai Chand Mukhopadhyay; artists such as Nandalal Bose and Anil Karanjai; and filmmakers such as Satyajit Ray. Indeed, one of the distinct pleasures of the book is how Roy incorporates the work and sensibilities of other artists as support and foil. None of these elements are without reason. This is intertextuality with purpose: deft, sharp, unforgettable.

Reading the book aloud offers an entrance into the world of the body. The lines are luscious in vowels; the narrative is often more complex than it appears. Later sections highlight the volatile intersections between visibility and survival through a continued focus on plant life. These sections are full of observation, sights, wonder. There is grief and resistance in this collection, threat and desire, impossible longing and devastating intimacy. Radicalism is rooted in earth, love, and community, a lesson Roy learns from watching plant life. Reading her work, I'm reminded of the etymology of the word 'watch': its roots in the Old English '*wæcc-*', or 'wake'. To watch is to wake, or be awake: to have one's eyes opened to another world, another level of consciousness. Roy's book ends on this note, "rejecting speed and excess". This is a work of resistance and hope.

A LESSON IN VISION

Review of Anything but Human *by Daryl Lim Wei Jie (Singapore: Landmark Books, 2021)*

Reviewed by Lydia Wei

During the 1960s, S. Rajaratnam, the first Culture and Foreign Minister of Singapore and the originator of the term "Singaporean Singapore," pronounced that to maintain Singaporean culture meant "forgetting all that stands in the way of one's Singaporean commitment." At the time of Singapore's conception, building a common culture for the nation seemed necessary. But as this work progressed, the nation began to forget more and more: to forget its history, to forget its lands, to forget its languages, its people, its crimes, its dreams—to forget until a large swath of truth and history was lost.

It is against this "total blankness of mind" that *Anything But Human* by Singaporean poet Daryl Lim Wei Jie operates. In an essay for the *Quarterly Literary Review Singapore*, Lim named Singapore's most heinous "original sin" as its intense proclivity to forget—and early in his collection, in the poem "Fly Forgotten, as a Dream (II)," Lim already references this original sin: "They taste deeply of the amnesia we've grown to love and cherish." Tingling on the tongue, the line shoulders both the burdens of Singapore's history and its potential for progress: How can we break out of this collective amnesia? When will we realize that the act of forgetting is unacceptable?

For a poet, images—lush and shocking, delivered directly or in metaphors, through rhythm and rhyme—are the foundational tools with which worlds are made. And when an entire nation is taught to forget any history that conflicts with its "Singaporean commitment," the only way it can attempt to understand itself is through the images and stories told by sanitized, sterilized mass media.

In *Anything But Human*, the images are cynical and distant. During what should be a picturesque picnic in "Fly Forgotten, as a Dream (VII)," all that appears are the excesses of our consumerism:

> *Plastic bottles strewn about us reflect your healthy nuclear glow. . . . In the background, sirens herald the arrival of a new age of deliciousness. You tell me to take out my microwaveable meal and start the picnic.*

Gone are the pastoral spaces, the bucolic wonders. Instead, nature is taken over by materialistic impulses—the dream of the picnic punctured and the plastic residue melting down the page. All the same, there is a detached quality to this scene: as the sirens blare in the background, we can imagine two figures, still picture-perfect with that "healthy nuclear glow," sprawled out on the blanket, still carrying on with the glossy image of the picnic. Is this resigned acceptance of the "new age of deliciousness" ironic or despairing? Though Lim critiques industrialism, the two figures of his poem fall in line with the macabre humor of the situation in which they find themselves, unable to move outside of it.

Lim continues his critique of consumerism and excess in "Narrative (II)," writing, "if you look closely the bushes / are growing plastic packaging." Nature itself is barely present in this "natural" world; we see only the pervasiveness of capital inhabiting the body of what was once natural. But is it possible for us to see something beyond this? Could there be another catalog of images?

The problem, of course, is that this specific set of images is one that has long been packaged and sold to us. It's what we've been inundated with in advertisements, on billboards, in catalogues, on screens. Even when we peer into nature, we can't see beyond the commercial image: our imaginations are restricted to that finite set of consumer lifestyles.

Lim captures this shrinkage poignantly in "Parkway": "There are acres of sleep we have not yet lost / and visions of paradise still not in the catalogue." Here, Lim bemoans the catalogue paradise of "[n]oodles from Sarawak, a newly discovered scent / from Azerbaijan, a tribal mask from London" created using factory labor, or the "acres of sleep" yet to be lost. What is horrifying, too, is the notion that all imagination is lost: without the sheen of the look, other "visions" of paradise can't even be seen. Both workers and consumers are lost to the images. And in "Narrative (IV)," the poet writes that upon "waking up, my lips mouth / designer brands." We know no respite from the onslaught of consumer culture, not even in dreams; our imagination is haunted by those perfectly curated vision-boards, pored over by marketing and exec teams in offices that reach the skies.

The consequences of consumerism's cultural stranglehold come to a head in "Monster," where Lim's surrealist brush paints a nightmarish portrait of mental degradation. Children—long viewed as guardians of imagination and symbols of the future—find themselves unable to distinguish between dreams and capital:

> The children, with lightbulbs for teeth, mistake
> their dreams for money
>
> Boiling garbage, they dream of foods
> made from refined flour and white sugar

"Foods / made from refined flour and white sugar" are mistaken for nutrition. But not only are images specifically processed, packaged, and publicized for us: they are just as easily wiped away from our eyes. In "Progress Updates," Lim reveals the Internet's violent, constant erasure of what we can see, learn, and do. Though we often think of the Internet as an open space where all knowledge can be shared and procured, Lim refutes such a belief:

> Wifi interferes
> with the flow of lyric
>
> and scallops me
> into a factor of production
>
> . . .
>
> Like the nation-state I am wiped clean
> of atrocities

Histories disappear. The nation-state, now liberated from foreign rule and seemingly "wiped clean of atrocities," forgets that its leaders were often complicit in colonialism. Those who would always have been in power remain in power. Meanwhile, the Internet stretches onward, infinite. The best we can hope for is that atrocities will live on in footnotes, but even that seems unlikely. The darkness at the edge of our field of vision draws nearer.

As our imaginations close tighter and tighter around a nucleus of consumerism and erasure, we realize, too, that our ability to pay attention—to view reality with an incisive eye—is not only blunted by these banalities of urban life, but actively forbidden. In "The vital impulse is this," Lim writes, "The smell of rain on a wet road is classified."

If the act of truly perceiving and experiencing life is prohibited, it should become all the more important. To cut through and see the grisly heart of life, to look past the glazed, glossy images, enables the poet to counter the collective amnesia of Singapore, that cultural blank slate, and to begin recording the histories of the nation as he knows them. Lim's collection itself, though, is less focused on the actual recording of histories, but more on beginnings: the first acknowledgement of the need for a new way of seeing. In "Catechism," the poet begins to recognize the necessity of vision with interiority. "I am an eye without an I," Lim writes. To be an eye that passively takes in marketed images—an eye without an I, without a self—isn't enough; the eye needs the discerning mind of the I to find the truth about the lying world.

And the poet shines when the eye and the I successfully come together: the subtle, surreal images in this book are the strength of *Anything But Human*. They insistently remind us to question the narratives given to us and to examine everything with the fullness of our beings. In "The Natural Order of Things," the poet refuses, amidst a mélange of grotesque images—from "sickness rising / from the laundry basket" to "gums bleed[ing] the colour of the moon"—to be swept up in a deluge of sensory overload. Instead, the poem ends with an insistent note that re-centers feeling and calls for a type of introspection that allows one to "just be." If sparrows flap out of "cytokine storm[s]" in the exterior world, then to even begin to seek understanding of one's interior world truly requires one to "just be careful":

> Things sometimes feel good, and sometimes
> not. Be careful, just be careful, will you, just be.

Similarly, in "Narrative (I)," sensations are grounded in the poet's body, centering the I within both the eye and the world at large. Some sensations seize the body "like a forest fire," and the natural world triggers the physical release of emotion:

> other days the slightest beauty
> razes through me like a forest fire
>
> today nothing but the sound of rain
> smothering my weeping

In both "The Natural Order of Things" and "Narrative (I)", the poet seems to wish to be left alone. Instead of consuming the same catalogs of images, instead of being told what to forget or what to remember by mass media, the poet aims to understand the world through his own physical experiences. The poet aims to feel both the intensity of what "razes through" them and the calmness of what simply "feel[s] good".

Observing reality through poetry is a form of remembering too: a way of recording images the way they were, not the way people will want them to be recorded; a way of preserving the truth, no matter how uncouth it is. In "New World Symphony," Lim writes:

I remember the generations   without access
                                                  to toilet paper

This is freedom from tyranny

This is a memory-palace   for those
                                                  unborn

To see reality—and to see the beauty amidst reality's ugliness, to believe in the possibility of "freedom" despite the suffering that came beforehand—also means to work towards a more powerful imagination. I often think back to a quote by the American artist and AIDS activist David Wojnarowicz, "We're being angry and complaining because we have to, but where we want to go is back to beauty. If you let go of that, we don't have anywhere to go." Lim, much like Wojnarowicz, is pointing towards a full embodiment of *envisioning*—that powerful combination of sight and imagination—that confronts all of life's harsh realities by mustering up the strength to imagine something more beautiful.

At any demand that you forget, at any demand that you consume only the images you're sold, *Anything But Human* asks that you push back. These poems demand a constant questioning, a constant insistence to see what needs to be seen. As Lim argues, the salvation for Singapore's original sin would be "more remembering and less forgetting"—a time to bear witness to and record more histories. In many ways, *Anything But Human* probes how a nation still young, with but 50 years of post-colonial history, may emerge from its collective amnesia and move forward. It reads like a lesson in vision. A portrait of sight.

A MOSQUE IN THE JUNGLE

Review of A Mosque in the Jungle: Classic Ghost Stories *by Othman Wok and edited by Ng Yi-Sheng (Singapore: Epigram Books, 2021)*

Reviewed by Sebastian Taylor

Modern stories of folk horror stem from "a backlash to industrial capitalism," argues Scott Benson, the video game designer. In his appearance on the *Spooky Town* podcast, he points out the persistent feeling in folk-horror stories that "there's a hidden structure under this [plot] . . . a machine that is turning." The ghost stories of Othman Wok, despite their varied surface detail, follow a similar structure: leading title, transgression, building tension, and then vengeance. The reader knows early on how most of the stories are going to end. Nevertheless, the reader feels a strong sense of horror because they have wandered into an ancient machine, or a "ruleset" as Benson calls it, that they and capitalism have displaced. There is an urge "to go back," Benson elaborates, but also a fear of discovering what has been repressed.

Othman Wok published his first horror stories in 1952 for the Malay paper *Utusan Zaman* in what was then called Malaya. *A Mosque in the Jungle* collects a selection of stories that Othman wrote for various newspaper columns between 1952 and 1987. During that period, Singapore left the newly formed postcolonial state of Malaysia and became an independent nation-state. The collection's editor Ng Yi-Sheng describes Othman in his introduction as a polyglot with his fingers in many pies. He was the minister of social affairs from 1963 to 1977. After he retired from politics, he served on the boards of the Singapore Tourism Board and Sentosa Development Corporation, the latter responsible for turning the southern island from a British military base and a Japanese prisoner-of-war camp into a popular tourist destination. From his vantage place, Othman saw, or perhaps oversaw, the rapid social and economic development of Singapore. His stories, I suggest, express the deep unease springing from the displacement of ancient, local knowledge by modern, global technologies.

Of the 24 stories in the collection, "Her Dead Husband Hasn't Left Home" is one such story that partly uncovers the mechanism Benson describes. This story, which Ng dubs as "uncannily autobiographical-sounding," follows the haunting of a student house in 1950s London. Instead of simply revealing the identity of the spirit, the title precipitates tension within the story. At first, the male narrator dismisses the eerie cold wind upon entering his room, "as drafts like this were common" in old houses. However, Mrs Bols, the landlady, suggests that "it may be the spirit of the house." The haunting remains tame compared to the horror of previous stories in the collection (such as "The Anklets"), but this tension between the knowledge of the narrator, landlady, and reader (whose knowledge is derived from the title) allows Othman to build up a profound uneasiness. The backstory of the spirit is not revealed until the end of the tale, when the author provides alternate interpretations of the haunting. From Mrs Bols' final reaction, the reader learns of a hidden knowledge she has kept throughout the tale. Despite the absence of gore, that horror feeling lies in the knowledge kept safe by a woman from a man, kept away by a landlady from a tenant, and lost almost irretrievably to the modern world.

These conflicting relationships to knowledge and power appear again in the story "The Skulls of Kuala Banat," written from the perspective of an English District Officer in the days of British colonialism. Officer Martin Haliday is slowly becoming obsessed with old European-style ruins in Kuala Banat. He aims to establish a new colony there, despite warnings from a local shaman, Pawang Mat Yassin. Folk knowledge comes into direct conflict with the knowledge of capital as all Martin Haliday "want[s] to do in his life [is] to be among the ruins, to live there and to work there." When Haliday tries to convince people to move to Kuala Banat, promising, "what a blessed land it [is] and what abundance it [offers]," his language focuses on economic resources and productivity, the exploitative concerns of imperial power. The resulting story is truly haunting in its resolution. The clash between folk and capital knowledge leaves the bystanders decimated. In the end, the only two survivors are the pawang and Haliday, the holders of conflicting knowledge. Othman himself is of Orang Laut origins with ties to the first peoples of Singapore and Malaysia. If we consider the sad colonial and postcolonial situation of the Orang Laut, this story becomes even more chilling.

Chilling, too, is reading "Si Hitam's Curse" and being reminded of "The Cats of Ulthar." The latter story was written by H. P. Lovecraft in 1920. Despite an eclectic writing style and a history of bigotry, Lovecraft still influences modern horror fiction. For example, Benson credits Lovecraft's story "From Beyond" for specific scenes in his 2017 video game *Night in the Woods*. It is interesting to consider how the different experiences of the three writers have contributed to a growing body of folk horror. Lovecraft drew from life in New England throughout the tumult of the first Red Scare and, later, the Great Depression. Othman, born in 1924, lived through the Japanese Occupation as well as the aftermath of British extractive capitalism. Benson, on the other hand, is still alive today and has drawn from the history of labour unions in the U.S. for his work. Despite these differences, the fiction of Othman, Lovecraft, and Benson cuts to the bone. "Si Hitam's Curse" and "The Cats of Ulthar" have similar plots, but they critically diverge in their portrayal of gendered violence.

"It is said that in Ulthar, which lies beyond the river Skai, no man may kill a cat," begins Lovecraft, because "[the cat] is more ancient than the Sphinx, and remembers that which she hath forgotten." Similarly, in "Si Hitam's Curse," the narrator's grandmother describes the cat, Si Hitam, as "descended from those the ancient kings of Bali used to keep," to justify the old Sanskrit-engraved collar the cat wears. Both descriptions stress the folk knowledge of respect for cats. Cats are an old species and are therefore connected to something larger than the narrators of both stories. In "The Cats of Ulthar," the special cat belongs to a young travelling boy, and his reliance on the cat is severed by "an old cotter and his wife who delighted to trap and slay the cats of their neighbours." In response, the boy's prayers are answered by the town's cats joining together to seek vengeance on the old couple.

The narrator of "Si Hitam's Curse" enacts similar violence on Si Hitam and her kitten; however, the cats' revenge is channelled through a woman rather than the cats themselves. The description of the violence is much more visceral than in Lovecraft's tale. In the latter, only picked-clean skeletons are left; whereas in the former, the culprit is found dead and "on his neck [is] a gaping wound, as if sharp teeth [have] sunk into it. Blood [is] spilled all over the mattress." The gore is exacerbated to reinforce the association of the female avenger with the cats. As such, the folk knowledge of royal cats is upheld through the women in the story. Othman seems to have transmuted Lovecraft's image of capital (signified by the disadvantaged position of the foreign and nomadic orphan boy) into a form of gendered knowledge. More generally Ng's selection of stories emphasizes this conflation of folk and female knowledge, an emphasis that may be lost in a less contemporary selection of Othman's work.

In his role as editor, Ng has arranged the stories so they progress "through both space and time." In his selection process, he has also assessed the effectiveness of Othman's stories to inspire dread. He explains that sometimes linguistic anachronisms distract from the horror of Wok's stories. A prizewinning poet and fiction writer, Ng has not translated the collection himself; he has only made minimal aesthetic edits to the translations while referring to the original Malay. In his introduction, Ng confesses that he does not consider himself qualified to re-translate the entire collection. Still, there remains some clumsiness in the resulting language of the book. In the story "Her Dead Husband Hasn't Left Home" the translation reads "more than forty years of age" in a description of a character. The formula sounds outdated. Then, in "Si Hitam's Curse," we read "Sweet Jamilah, a fellow student at the university, with whom I had fallen in love." The overly formal placement of the preposition "with" can be off-putting. Arguably, such archaisms situate the contemporary reader in relation to the text, reminding the reader that the stories are old. In a way, the clunky translation preserves some of the old tensions of 1950s Singapore: the toll of rapid modernisation, the dismantling of indigenous autonomy, and the new spaces and language of gendered violence, for example.

I did not know what to expect when I first began reading this book. It had the potential to be a monster-of-the-week collection, or perhaps a collection of cautionary tales. Instead, what I found was a timeless mélange of surprisingly modern anxieties trapped inside Scott Benson's "hidden machine." Though the language, or more specifically the syntax, feels archaic at times, the editor has chosen and arranged the stories well. Ng hopes "that this publication will prompt others in the future to delve deeper into Singaporean, Malaysian and Malayan literary history." It is my opinion that this collection of stories does just this, exploring knowledge that is both *of* and *for* the modern world.

A SET OF DIFFERENCES AND RELATIONS

Review of Pearls from Their Mouth *by Pear Nuallak (UK: Hajar Press, 2022)*

Reviewed by Jiaqi Kang

I always say, sort of jokingly but also very seriously, that if the apocalypse were to come, I would simply lie down and pass away. I can imagine both the end of the world *and* the end of capitalism—they'll probably happen together—but it's what comes next that fills me with uncertainty. When we've outrun the zombies and flash floods and have made a precarious home out of an abandoned schoolhouse, will we remember to be kind to one another? To pay attention, to be generous, to deal healthily with conflict? Will we build that better world we dream of, one without police, without prisons, without borders, without ableism and bigotry, without needless cruelty and greed?

Pear Nuallak offers a nuanced set of responses to these questions in their debut book, *Pearls from Their Mouth*. In this collection of fiction and essays from Hajar Press, a new UK-based independent publisher of books by and for people of color, Nuallak shows there is no perfect model for the future, even when one has all the 'correct' politics. To push it further: what is it that we seek when we search for easy, neat answers to tricky political questions? A sense of comfort? Permission to be complacent? A handing over of responsibility? A reason to look down on those who are ignorant? Nuallak suggests that answers can arise only from taking action: from delighting in the unexpected and the surprising, and letting our politics be enriched by practice.

Take 'Fifth Finger, Left Hand', the first of five fictional pieces in *Pearls from Their Mouth*. In this story, a pair of kinnaree (winged supernatural beings who can travel between worlds) from the Himmapan Forest live as humans in the modern world. The older sister, Ploy, marries a white man to immigrate from Thailand to the UK, leaving her unnamed younger sibling behind. Years later, Ploy escapes her husband and builds a Sanctuary in "the watery space between realms" where vulnerable women pay for safe shelter by giving up their memories. It is to this seemingly utopian space that Ploy brings the person she insists on calling her little sister. But the sibling, who has spent years searching for Ploy and is initially thrilled to be reunited with her, must face the realization that Ploy "is a stranger": she believes her guardianship and power give her the right to override the agency of those under her protection, namely by coercing people to trade their memories for safety, without explaining the consequences of such a loss. Ploy denies that her sibling, her partner, and her guests all might chafe under her imposed authority, and she justifies herself by insisting she is a better alternative to the violence of the (British) state: "You know, at other places, people are made to recite their traumas repeatedly to access help. We're different," Ploy says. In the end, her sibling decides to leave the Sanctuary to live on their own terms.

Moving between different characters' perspectives, 'Fifth Finger, Left Hand' initially establishes a conventional premise involving sisterhood, migration, and motherland. But Nuallak quickly undoes the reader's expectations by letting the complexities of life into the Sanctuary, asking questions like: Who is 'woman', and how are the borders of womanhood policed? Does our pain and trauma define us? What is the best way to help others? To what extent are all relationships transactional? Can broken systems be reformed from the inside? It is natural to make mistakes, but Ploy's fatal flaw is her unwillingness to change, which turns her 'safe space' into a festering wound. All of this suggests to the reader that even the best-intentioned initiatives can falter if power is not distributed equally, and being a marginalized person who cares for fellow marginalized people does not shield one from criticism.

Another of Nuallak's stories that stood out to me was 'Skin Like Sunlight Through Water', which explores the codependent relationship between a mother and daughter. The daughter, Thames, struggles to be her authentic queer self, fearing that to assert her own personhood would be to betray her mother, Nipah. "If I was a better daughter I could handle it," Thames says of Nipah's constant violations of her boundaries.

This deeply personal immigrant dilemma feels all too familiar to me. It was also the central theme of the recent Asian American science fiction film *Everything Everywhere All at Once* (2022). In the movie, a mother and her queer daughter, played by Michelle Yeoh and Stephanie Hsu respectively, fight each other across parallel universes but ultimately reconcile through a conversation in the parking lot outside their Laundromat. Yeoh's character learns to accept her daughter's girlfriend into the family and to live a content life not ruled by disappointment and what-ifs.

While 'Skin Like Sunlight Through Water' also uses speculative elements (in this case, an app that allows dream-sharing) as a channel for its emotional arc, Nuallak refuses to hand us such a simple resolution. The penultimate scene in Nuallak's story shows Nipah visiting Thames's dream and seeing her converse with her queer friends, whose influence Nipah feels will corrupt her daughter. Enraged, anxious, and confused, Nipah brings a flood into the dream; as the others flee and the water crashes down upon Thames, "she is completely still, floating." Nipah's journey to recognition of, and accountability for, her treatment of Thames is a long and nonlinear one that stretches beyond the end of the story. This open-ended, unconventional approach to conflict stands in contrast to *Everything Everywhere All at Once*, which, as British journalist Ian Wang writes, "is teleologically structured around that final reconciliatory conversation," as though one conversation could be so meaningful as to soothe the pain of many lifetimes.

It's also apt to bring up *Everything Everywhere All at Once* here because of the way that movie—like any movie with Asian cast members—inevitably raises broader questions about representation. What is 'good' or 'correct' representation? Were any cultures appropriated in the making of this film? Were communities empowered? RepresentAsian (meaning Asian representation in media and society, but also sometimes used to describe an Asian person who cares only about such representation) is a central issue in *Pearls from Their Mouth*. RepresentAsians believe that mainstream visibility—manifested through movie stars and CEOs who 'look like us'—might bring individuals a sense of validation and belonging. Such an idea suggests that the feeling of having one's identity confirmed is the key to ending oppression, which masks material issues like housing discrimination and immigration rights. Part of what makes Nuallak's book so strong compared to the typical Instagram infographic on 'stopping Asian hate' is its rejection of RepresentAsian's shallow, perhaps counter-productive contribution to activism.

RepresentAsian is insidious because it presents Asians as a monolith and erases the experiences of Asians who are not poster children for white Western acceptance: undocumented people, sex workers, dark-skinned people, anyone who makes 'us' look 'bad'. As Nuallak aptly puts it, RepresentAsian "remains an essentially neoliberal project. To the RepresentAsian activists, the problem is not capitalism but rather that ESEAs [editor: East and Southeast Asians] do not feature more prominently among the higher rungs of its hierarchy." This lack of desire to interrogate the capitalist system that undergirds racism is especially apparent when we examine the subtle anti-Blackness of much RepresentAsian struggle against Asian 'invisibility'. Responses like 'If they'd said the N-word, people would be mad, but when it's against Asians . . .' not only completely dismiss the Black struggle but also overwrite the fact that Asian and Black histories are entangled and that it makes no sense to see Black and Asian liberation as separate.

Similarly, Nuallak's discussion of transphobia and queer politics is sharp yet patient, unyielding yet considerate. In 'Ancestor, Trancestor', one of the issues Nuallak tackles is the question of what it means for trans-people to dig through the past for icons to venerate. Considering that gender and sex have been constructed and maintained socially in vastly different ways across human history, it can be difficult for us to productively label certain figures as trans. But perhaps we seek to use history to establish a sense of legitimacy, a justification for our existence today, 'trancestors' paving the way for future assimilation and acceptance. Perhaps we are imagining a bygone time when life was better and safer for trans-people.

Either way, the impulse to create trancestors seems to be driven by the idea that capital-H History (or even Herstory) makes community. But the writing of History is determined by power relations, where certain icons are elevated to national mythology at the expense of alternative, not-so-neat, smaller-scale stories. Nuallak writes, "It should concern us when community is turned into a symbol, thin as a coin, rather than a set of differences and relations we make through joyful and difficult struggle." At the end of the day, Nuallak reminds us, "If we want to bring up Marsha P. Johnson, Sylvia Rivera, Stormé DeLarverie, Miss Major or any other historical icon, then it should be to remind ourselves of how we need to act, *care as not just feeling but as action*; transness as action; art as action." (My emphasis.) Care-as-action can bring us together. Togetherness should come from a place of radical inclusion, not the suspicious exclusion on which the nation-state builds itself. "We dream of a Queer Nation," Nuallak concludes in this passage, playing on the name of an activist group from 1990s New York, "but the Nation is what we must destroy."

Nuallak's fiction is full of symbols, which frequently makes it come off as heavy-handed. In part due to their brevity, the stories in *Pearls from Their Mouth* are burdened with allegory; every incident, every dynamic must not only succeed within the narrative but also represent a real-world dilemma with all its contradictions and complexities. This desire for every fictional piece to contain lessons or pointers also means that Nuallak sometimes prioritizes such themes over aesthetics and craft. For instance, their characters' important internal shifts are sometimes just stated outright. In 'Fifth Finger, Left Hand', Ploy's sibling decides to leave the Sanctuary by thinking to themself: "I used to think finding my sister would complete me, but only I can do that. Her real gift to me has been a new sense of clarity, and I will allow myself to be grateful for this." In 'Skin Like Sunlight Through Water', Nipah is comforted by her more open-minded friend, who "murmur[s] things that she [Nipah] needs to hear but struggles to accept." Were these stories longer, the reader might be able to come to their own understanding without such shortcuts.

At the end of the day, this book is an act of propaganda—at which Nuallak succeeds, especially through their combination of allegorical fiction with nonfiction pieces. *Pearls from Their Mouth* is an unapologetically political work of art, not so much a call-to-arms (as that would be too simple) but a book dedicated to an audience already at arms, whose arms are sore but who are keen to keep fighting. It's a book that holds its reader in high esteem, that is, it speaks clearly and straightforwardly without talking down. "Contrary to popular narratives about the motivations of racialised queer authors, I write with the presumption of your disagreement and confusion," Nuallak says in one essay, "not with the expectation of speaking into an echo chamber." It's unclear exactly how Nuallak expects the reader to feel "confusion" here, because the book as a whole strives for clarity, sometimes to its own narrative detriment; perhaps they do not wish to over-explain their own racialised queer life experiences for the sake of entertainment. But I appreciate the provocation behind the sentence and the rejection of the idea that political discussion should be perfectly comfortable. This approach is what forms the basis of solidarity, of comradeship in political work: We don't have to agree on everything. All we need is to trust that others care as much as we do. The rest will come.

IN HER LIGHT

Review of In the Same Light: 200 Tang Poems for Our Century *by Wong May (UK: Carcanet, 2022)*

Reviewed by Kevin Tsai

If 19th-century metrical renditions made the best Tang authors sound sentimental and unremarkable, 20th-century translations brought about a radical reassessment by foregrounding the imagistic, evocative qualities of Chinese poetry. Translators such as Pound, Rexroth, Williams, and others even inspired new directions in American poetry. Lacking a command of classical Chinese, many relied on a native informant whose words they recast as verse. The 21st-century calls for the natives to speak, for poets of Asian descent to address this asymmetrical division of labor. Wong May's anthology *In the Same Light: 200 Tang Poems for Our Century* is a welcome contribution, and it should invite us to consider the balance between fidelity and beauty in interpreting another culture.

A translator cannot avoid sounding at least somewhat like herself. An anthology, with multiple voices, amplifies the problem. How does one convey Du Fu's reliance on allusion and unconventional syntax or set Bo Juyi's plain language against Li Shangyin's thorny diction? In a sense this collection treats not 30+ individual poets, but a particular conception of poetry, for it is hard to distinguish individual voices. In many of these translations, detached, playful lines are often sharply interrupted by notes of emotional depth, creating moments of drama rather than disconnection. Each poem seems to evolve an architecture of its own, often reflecting Wong May's technique rather than something in the original. Here, as in her own poetry, her style is spare and sensual at the same time. Indeed, it really feels like all these poets are seen *In the Same Light*. They are all Wong May.

This is not necessarily bad. Wong May's own poetry favors shorter lines, using line breaks and indents to organize meaning and emotion. In this anthology, she deploys these tools quite effectively to translate a tradition in which meaning often depends on structure. Rather than attempting to convey the structure of the original as does David Hinton or William Carlos Williams, Wong May often creates a new, loose structure that makes visible an organization, if only a local one. Below is an example that illustrates a few structuring principles and their differences in the style of translation. He Zhizhang's poem on homecoming is a septasyllabic quatrain in which each one of the four lines has a specific function: namely, "begin, continue, turn, and close" (*qi cheng zhuan he*). Williams's translation shows this structure well:

> Returning after I left my home in childhood,
> I have kept my native accent but not the color of my hair.
> Facing the smiling children who shyly approach me,
> I am asked from where I come.

The quatrain structure invites the reader to consider the situation in the first half in light of the scene in the second half. But Wong May breaks the first two lines, making four lines that suggest some sort of contrast and parallel, losing the quatrain structure and rhythm altogether.

Left home—a young man,

    —am yet to lose the accent.

The thinning hair,

    Must have made an impression;

Village kids gawk & giggle

Wanting to know where I'm from.

Though this strategy seems to abandon one type of structure, it is inspired by another type. In the original, the first two lines contrast the past with the present in something called an "antithesis," whereby parts of a line correspond to parts of the other line in a couplet. Below is not a translation, but a glossary for the purpose of illustration.

shao	xiao	li	jia		lao	da	hui
少	小	離	家		老	大	回
[in youth		leaves home]			[in maturity returns]		

xiang	yin	wu	gai		bin	mao	shuai
鄉	音	無	改		鬢	毛	衰
[accent		not changed]			[hair at the temples declines]		

"In youth leaves home" in line 1 corresponds to "accent not changed" in line 2, and this contrast suggests the stability of identity in spite of the circumstances. "In maturity returns" in line 1 resonates with "hair at the temples declines" in line 2. Such correspondences may seem somewhat arbitrary in English, but in the original Chinese they are very clear and neat in terms of syllable count, position in the line, and often even parts of speech. Wong May's reorganization cuts short the work of antithesis, in the process deleting a phrase in favor of something she invents.

Remaking the structure, drawing inspiration from ideas she sees in the original, is a strategy Wong May uses throughout. Sometimes the result is amazing. Luo Binwang's "Goose" seems impossible to translate well because what makes it work is the antithesis, which sounds stifling in English. Wong May breaks it up into a series of stanzas reminiscent of the wake of a goose in a pond and creates the fragmentary lines to do the job of rigid structure.

Indeed, this volume is not shy about making heavy-handed intervention, and there is often a significant gap between the literal meaning and the translation of each line. For example, the final line of Meng Haoran's "Spring Dawn," "Who knows how many flowers have fallen?" is rendered "You do not ask / What flowers / There were / What / Still to fall." This reinvention highlights the question invisible in the literal translation: what is the state of things? Wong May is a "translator traitor," and although most instances of "betrayal" seem like deliberate choices, occasionally a line surfaces that appears suspect. In Du Fu's famous poem about his war-ravaged homeland, Wong May offers: "Flowers are seen in tears," which makes one wonder whether *jian* ("to see") has been confused with its homophone *jian* (a different character meaning "to splash") in the original. In the larger context a dynamic moment of sensing emotions—splashing a flower with tears—is transformed into something more static. But this could very well be a "purposeful mistake," as in her translation of Liu Zongyuan's poem that references one's inner "nature" (*xing*), a key concept in Buddhism. Wong May chooses to capitalize it, making it into the thing with trees and mountains (not what *xing* means), and reinvents the rest of the line to confess her trick: "vanished Nature / May even / Be found back in us."

Sometimes Wong May fabricates a line outright. The final poem, by the prolific author Anonymous, concludes with a powerful punch: "Ceaseless // Forgive." Though there is just no trace of it in the original, the poem is better for it. In other words, whether it is a small modification or an invention, she makes it work, and she may even need it for the poem to work because of her aesthetics. Perhaps a good summation of her approach to translation is Li Shangyin's "Silk Zither," the final four lines of which she renders as:

> High sea.　　　　Bright moon.
> Pearl-fishers come back up with tears.
>
> Blue fields.　　　　Warm sun.
> Smoke
> 　　　Rises
> Where
> 　　　Jade lies buried,
>
> 　　　Fat of some land;
>
> Memory
> What have you held back?
>
> You do not speak.
>
> Unbidden
> The zither gives no notice.
>
> We were clueless then
>
> It's all that's left us now.

The first two stanzas begin to suggest a parallel structure, only to devolve into an alternate arrangement where the English is only loosely inspired by the Chinese. The translation tries again at some sort of pattern with "Memory" and "Unbidden," but again devolves into a spare line—one of the translator's own inventions here—to conclude the poem. This is not how one would expect to handle the straitjacket form of Li Shangyin's regulated verse. For comparison, David Young gives

full moon above the ocean
pearls swelling in a sea of tears

the sun grows warm—in indigo pastures
fine jade begins to smoke

love should live on and on
filling our years and memories

but somehow it dazes us, fading,
and we're not even sure it was real.

What is translated in the two renditions above as "blue fields" or "indigo pastures" refers to a mountain, which is also called Jade Mountain. Both of these names are used in a single line in the original. The scene is just a mountain smoking under the heat of the sun, and not anything surreal as Young's translation suggests. A third translation, by David Hinton (below), is more grounded in the original. Note that he uses enjambment to avoid the static rigidity that the Chinese form may have in English.

. . . moonlight on vast seas—it's pearl's tear:
far off, Indigo Mountain jade smokes in warm sun: up close,

smoke vanishes: can this feeling linger even in a memory:
never anything but this moment already bewildered and lost.

These three translations offer quite a range of interpretations. Young captures the quiet intensity. Hinton is closest to the Tang poet in structure and meaning, but feels somewhat legato and wordy. Wong May captures the rhythm, energy, and the haunting feeling better. In the Afterword, she speaks of "poetry [arising] independently of words; not what is said, but what it does to you." Here her translation punches hard in the silence between the lines, and it feels as visceral as Li Shangyin, though by inventing eight lines that would have surprised him. For comparison, the original lines corresponding to the quoted translations are:

滄海月明珠有淚，藍田日暖玉生煙。
此情可待成追憶？只是當時已惘然。

In this anthology, there is something that sounds eerily right, and also something that sounds eerily wrong, because Wong May gets things right by being wrong, and wrong by being right. Contemporary readers do not always appreciate the formal beauty, restraint, and allusive labyrinth of classical Chinese poetry, and most translators adopt simpler, less puffed-up language: witness David Young's approachable *Five T'ang Poets* (1990). Such avoidance of complexity, combined with Wong May's creative structure and inventive lines, gives her contemporary translations a different appearance. Scholars will probably not like it. And yet the emotional texture is sometimes just so recognizable: embedded within is a soul renewed for our times. The reader will have to decide for himself at what point the ship of Theseus remains the ship of Theseus, and at what point it ought to be regarded as the creation of the repairman. But perhaps a deeper question is: is it fair that translators of classical Chinese often have to strip away cultural depth, whereas those working on classical Greek and Latin do not have to do so as much?

By contrast to Wong May's admirable craft, her poem selection leaves something to be desired. Thanks to the outsized influence of the schoolboy anthology *300 Tang Poems* (1763), translators of Chinese poetry often focus on a small body of works, giving rise to, say, *Nineteen Ways of Looking at Wang Wei* (1987) and few ways of looking at the rest of the vast corpus. From the Tang Dynasty alone, there are over 48,900 poems, and it would do Anglophone readers a great service to introduce a more diverse sampling. Many poems in the present anthology are well-known and well-served in existing translations. Perhaps the selection reflects the translator's sense of kinship with the "migrants and exiles" of the Tang Dynasty, as the dedication says, but most of these poets "migrated" or were exiled because they belonged to an elite who might encounter such misfortunes in their government careers. These circumstances are hard to compare to those of today's economic migrants and refugees.

Finally, *In the Same Light* does not do enough to help the reader comprehend the context, which can be crucial for poems from another culture and time period. Although the afterword, occupying 100 pages, speaks of the "social-historical context," readers looking for an introduction to Chinese poetry should search elsewhere. They might consult exemplary guides such as Zong-qi Cai's *How to Read Chinese Poetry* (2007), which offers the Chinese characters, transliteration, glossary, literal translation, and scholarly introduction to each genre and analysis of each poem. This anthology's afterword is creative, playful, idiosyncratic, and not organized, and it should be regarded as a poetic statement combined with notes and thoughts from the writing of the book. For example, it asserts hyperbolically that birds and tears are prevalent in Chinese poetry, but in truth such imagery applies only to a narrow range of works. At times the afterword makes speculations based on incomplete information. Wong May surmises that Tang poets writing in women's voices could be explained as "gender fluidity" or as a "gallant" defense of the oppressed sex, but such an explanation misses the full picture as these works do follow a long tradition of male writers projecting patriarchal fantasies on women. This is not "gotcha," but just the recognition that because the afterword is meant for those in the know, it is not useful for the general reader who is unequipped to deduce, say, why the Huang Chao's massacre in Chang'an "rightly" began with the scholar-officials.

This volume really should have used a copyeditor familiar with Chinese. Below is not an exhaustive list. The names of the poets are sometimes incorrectly and even inconsistently spelled; e.g., Meng Haoran appears as "Meng Hao Ren" (p. 9, Table of Contents) and as "Meng Haran" (p. 299); Luo Binwang appears as "Luo Bin Wang" (TOC) and as "Luo Bingwang" (p. 295). "Du Fu," given in *pinyin* romanization in the TOC, appears twice as "Tu Fu" (p. 93) in Wade-Giles romanization, giving the impression these are two different people. Sometimes different romanization systems are mixed up in the same word; e.g., the *Book of Poetry* should be either "*Shijing*" (*pinyin*) or "*Shih-ching*" (W-G), and not a combination of the two ("*Shih-Jing*," p. 330). The afterword often capitalizes Chinese terms, forgetting that is done in English only for proper names, not for basic words such as "civilization" or "benevolence" (which should be "*wenming*" and "*ren*" rather than "*Wen-Ming*," p. 325, and "*Ren*," p. 346). There are also outright mistakes: e.g., *zhu shen* for "*chu shen*" (p. 303) or "*jui-lian*" (p. 343) and later "*jiu-lian*" (p. 344) for "*julian*." Romanization may seem like a small matter, but such carelessness can really confuse readers. Sometimes historical figures are given names difficult to recognize. Emperor Taizu of Later Liang appears as

"Emperor Quangzong" (p. 337) which uses a slightly misspelled version of his given name (Quanzhong, family name Zhu). No Chinese emperor ever went by their given name. There are also regular typographical errors in the afterword.

Quoted Translations

William Carlos Williams's translation in *The New Directions Anthology of Classical Chinese Poetry*, ed. E. Weinberger (New Directions, 2003), p. 60.

David Young, trans. & ed., *Five T'ang Poets* (Oberlin, 1990), p. 167.

David Hinton, trans. & ed., *Classical Chinese Poetry* (Farrar, Straus and Giroux, 2008), p. 310.

A RECKONING WITH READING

Review of Bibliolepsy: A Novel *by Gina Apostol (USA: Soho Press, January 2022)*

Reviewed by Diane Josefowicz

I was fourteen when, in 1986, Corazon Aquino was elected president of the Philippines after months of mass protests against Ferdinand Marcos and his regime. As I watched the demonstrations, a thread of sympathy flew from my suburban backwater in Rhode Island to Quezon City and Manila. Yellow was the color of the People Power Revolution; on TV, it was everywhere.

In other words, I fell in love with signs, having zero understanding of the realities that produced them. All I actually knew about the Philippines was Marcos was a hateful kleptocratic dictator and that his wife, Imelda, owned a lot of shoes. Although this latter detail is both puerile and irrelevant to the significance of Aquino's ascendancy, it is germane to my reading of Gina Apostol's new novel, *Bibliolepsy*. This hilarious romp through the end of the Marcos regime is unsettlingly pervaded by the topsy-turvy logic of accumulation, particularly of signs. That this accumulation has its pleasures is, Apostol suggests, something we still need to reckon with.

Written in the 1980s, the novel is a coming-of-age story in which a student, Primi Peregrino, grows from innocence to experience by means of literature, or more precisely, her erotic involvements with men who write it. An exceptionally devout reader, Primi notches her belt with romantic conquests she makes in bookstores and libraries. A bookshelf is her Tinder. When Primi is swept into the protests that oust Marcos and bring Aquino to power, she finds herself unmoved. She is a deeply literate erotic adventurer with a front-row seat at a revolution—and it interests her less than books and sex.

How Primi developed her kink occupies the novel's first part, in which Apostol weaves literary concerns, including plenty of unabashedly poststructuralist wordplay, with raunchily funny sex scenes. Primi is initiated into the joys of reading when she discovers a trove of pornography owned by her father, a writer and illustrator of comic books. What Primi lacks in knowledge, older sister Annie happily supplies. "What's fellatio, Annie?" she asks. Annie replies, "Hm. It sounds like an illness." Together they look it up in the *OED*. "It impressed me then . . . that this word had been used in ancient times, 1887, what a long time ago, when people didn't have much to talk about most probably," Primi deadpans, "and they thought about fellatio." The next word Primi looks up is *penis*. Her excursions into the etymology of gross and sexy things conclude with an admonition from her grandmother that reading (reading!) will make her blind.

Primi's bibliolepsy is partly an homage to her parents. Her father, I've said, was a writer of comic books; her mother, a nervous taxidermist who calmed herself by repeating the names of bones, bodies of water, and the cities of the Philippine archipelago. These two care about signs, about how meaning circulates in social and political systems. Bedding writers is a way of belonging to this family of offbeat semioticians. But it also represents a bid for independence. Primi's parents are dissidents who disappear; they are, perhaps, assassinated. This is heavy stuff, but Primi tires of the freightedness of politics. She breaks with her family by becoming intellectually light, voluble, virtually nonpolitical—a fan.

Literature engages Primi, but what she likes is literalism. Her idea of close reading is about as close as you can get. One of her lovers, Vincent Sabado, was "unknown to me at first," she reports. What she means is that she hasn't read him. So how does she get to know him? Not by speaking with him, as we might expect—instead, *she reads all his books.* This is pathetic; it is also very funny. Apostol is a brilliant comic writer, and *Bibliolepsy* is full of pleasurably gut-busting moments like this one.

But is pleasure enough? Vaguely concerned to marry politics and desire, Primi has intuitions about how "the plot of desire" might converge with other plots. But these concerns remain abstract. As a reader, Primi wants out of politics and the history it creates. "It's not easy to live within a novel," she says of the protests. "One does not wish to lie awash, willy-nilly, within the commanding stream of another's story. . . . I'd felt the need to move out of fate's fast-moving pen . . . to jump off history's inexorably written text, the truck of time, and fall into a ravine of my own choosing." For Primi, this escape is "the promise of sex and love—and the readings that go with them: the thrill of a moment's stalled flesh, while the rest of the world whizzes by." Her escapism has all the ambiguous attraction of an ad for an all-inclusive resort vacation, which might be paradise—or it might just be boring.

To make sense of her discomfort, Primi stacks up authors and tropes. To convey her sense of herself as a "vagabond from history," Primi makes references to a whole series of figures, from Heraclitus to the Wandering Jew. But when everything seems relevant, it's hard to know how anything is. She describes the People Power Revolution as "this wind-rushed tale of 1986," blithely drawing an equivalence with Britain's Windrush generation, even though the *Empire Windrush's* passengers were caught up in a very different process. Eventually even Primi loses patience with glib symbolic transformations: "The time comes with you get tired of getting manipulated atop poem manuscripts and look for more piercing engagements." She returns to the bookstore, only to suffer buyer's remorse. "I flit from one book to another, take up three or four at a time. . . . Then I return home with this odd assortment. My bookshelf is filled with evidence of my sudden fancies and the stupid eclectic objects of my lust. Afterwards I don't remember why I had brought them home."

Primi is not alone in her faith that owning yet another object of desire will transform a difficult reality. A genius list-maker, Apostol shares something of Primi's ethos, but Apostol's tongue-in-cheek collections of detail function more critically and subversively. While Primi accumulates books and lovers to no effect, Apostol piles details into grand heaps in order to upend them. She keeps the reader on her toes. In Primi I recognize the temptation to seek salvation in accumulation. As I write amidst heaps of books, I think of Mrs. Marcos and her staggering collection of shoes. My present reverence for my library does not cohere at all with my past contempt for her closet. Something has to give. But as I read Apostol, I wonder if that's her point: our understandings of events are not stable, and as meanings shift, new possibilities arise that we might improve upon or not, depending. *Hypocrite lecteur, mon semblable, ma soeur!*

ABOUT THE AUTHORS

Aniruddh was a Bhojpuri poet hailing from Maker in the Saran district of Bihar. His poetry features rich yet poised depiction of rustic, idyllic rural life and calm reflection on the day-to-day activities of ordinary village-folk. He is best-known for his work 'Panihaarin'. This poem "N āv Khule M ānjh ī Re" juxtaposes the spiritual theme of transcendence with an everyday setting and common, lay sights through the use of extended metaphor. Aniruddh was born in Dihi village, which lay on the banks of the River Gandak. His childhood was spent in an idyllic, verdant, and picturesque setting, which is reflected in the prominence of natural themes in his poetry. Rural themes both feature directly as well as retain a strong influence conveyed through motifs in his works. Aniruddh was an active participant in sociocultural circles, events, and activities. Known for being a humble and genial samaritan, he took initiative in organising grassroots literary events at the local level and furthering the intellectual and literary cause in his community.

Oral Arukenova is a poet, literary critic, and translator. She studied the German language in Almaty and business management in Hamburg. Her stories, poems, and articles have been published in literary journals in Kazakhstan, Russia, Germany, and the United States, including in *Brooklyn Rail* and the forthcoming anthology *Amanat*.

Anastasiya Belousova was born in Almaty in 1996. She has a master's degree in specialized literary studies and is a graduate of the program for poetry, prose, and children's literature at the Open Literature School of Almaty.

Minxi Chua (she/her) is a writer, editor, and filmmaker from Kuala Lumpur. She is currently based in Bristol, and pursuing an MA in Creative Writing at Brunel University. Her work centers on her lived experiences as a queer Chinese Malaysian woman and explores themes of madness and magic.

Shelley Fairweather-Vega is a professional translator of Russian and Uzbek in Seattle, Washington. She translates poetry, fiction, screenplays and more for authors around the world, with a special focus on the contemporary literature of Uzbekistan and Kazakhstan. Fairweather-Vega holds degrees in International Relations and Russian, East European, and Central Asian Studies. As a translator, she is most interested in the intersection of culture and politics in modern history. Her published projects and work in progress are at fairvega.com/translation.

Sigrid Marianne Gayangos was born and raised in Zamboanga City, Philippines. Her works have appeared in various venues such as *Cha: An Asian Literary Journal, Ombak: Southeast Asia's Weird Fiction Journal, ANMLY, Likhaan Journal, Everything Change: An Anthology of Climate Fiction and Reckoning Magazine*, among others. Her debut collection of short stories, *Laut*, is forthcoming from the University of the Philippines Press.

Irina Gumyrkina was born in 1987 in eastern Kazakhstan. She completed the poetry seminar at the Open Literature School of Almaty and works as a journalist and editor. Gumyrkina has published her poetry in the journals *Plavuchy most, Prostor, Etazhi, Zvezda*, and more, and is the author of two books of poetry.

Atar Hadari trained as an actor before studying playwriting with Derek Walcott at Boston University. His plays have won awards from the BBC, Arts Council of England, National Foundation of Jewish Culture (New York), European Association of Jewish Culture (Brussels), and the RSC, where he was Young Writer in Residence. His plays have been staged at Finborough Theatre, Wimbledon Studio Theatre, Chichester Festival Theatre, Mark Taper Forum, and West Yorkshire Playhouse. His sitcom script "Strictly Kosher" won an Alfred Bradley award from the BBC. His *Songs from Bialik: Selected Poems of H. N. Bialik* (Syracuse University Press) was a finalist for the American Literary Translators' Association Award. His first poetry collection *Rembrandt's Bible* was published by Indigo Dreams. The PEN Translates award—winning *Lives of the Dead: Collected Poems of Hanoch Levin* is out now from Arc Publications.

Chris Huntington is the author of the prizewinning novel *Mike Tyson Slept Here*. His nonfiction has appeared in numerous anthologies and outlets, including National Public Radio and the *New York Times*. His poetry has been featured in *Rattle, Solstice, Peatsmoke, Singapore Unbound*, and elsewhere. More information is available at www.chrishuntingtononline.com.

The intimate works of visual and performance artist **ila** (she/her, Singapore) incorporate objects, moving images, and live performance. Through weaving imagined narratives into existing realities, she seeks to create alternative nodes of experience and entry points into the peripheries of the unspoken, the tacit, and the silenced. Using her body as a space of tension, negotiation, and confrontation, her works generate discussion about gender, history, and identity, in relation to pressing contemporary issues. She writes speculative fiction and is working on a collection of shorts, *Pura-Pura Parade*.

Diane Josefowicz is reviews editor at *Necessary Fiction*. Her debut novel *Ready, Set, Oh* was published in May 2022, by Flexible Press.

Jiaqi Kang is the founding editor-in-chief of *Sine Theta Magazine*, an international, print-based publication made by and for the Sino diaspora. They are a doctoral student in art history, researching hygiene politics in postsocialist Chinese art. Their fiction has been listed on the Wigleaf Top 50 2022. Find them online: jiaqikang.carrd.co.

Pitamber Kaushik is a writer, columnist, teacher, and independent researcher. His writings, cutting across boundaries of disciplines, styles, and geopolity, have appeared in over a hundred publications across thirty-five countries. He is interested in exploring philosophy, politics, linguistics, social psyche, and culture through his creative efforts, focussing on rationalism, postcolonialism, environmentalism, and social justice, among others. With his interdisciplinary, comparative, and eclectic approach to the humanities, he considers himself a xenophile—a purveyor and philatelist of unique ideas and historico-cultural curios.

Ayesha Khan (she/her) is based out of a town in Himachal Pradesh, India. She works as an Assistant Professor of English Literature. She writes in English and Urdu, neither of which is her first language. Twitter @aayeshaa_khan

Khashayar "Kess" Mohammadi (He/They) is a queer, Iranian-born, Toronto-based poet, writer, and translator. Shortlisted for the 2021 Austin Clarke Poetry Prize, they are the winner of the 2021 Vallum Poetry Prize and the author of three poetry chapbooks and two translated poetry chapbooks. Their debut poetry collection *Me, You, Then Snow* is out with Gordon Hill

Press. Their second book *WJD* is forthcoming in a double volume with the translation of Saeed Tavanaee's *The OceanDweller* from Gordon Hill Press in Fall 2022. Their collaborative poetry manuscript with poet Klara Du Plessis is forthcoming with Palimpsest Press in Fall 2023.

Monica Kim is a queer writer and organizer. Born in South Korea, she now lives in Brooklyn, New York. She won the inaugural Jane Kenyon Chapbook Prize Award in 2020 and the *Blue Mountain Review* Asian American Poetry Chapbook Contest in 2021. Her writing has been published in *A Velvet Giant, Call Me [Brackets], Pollux Journal,* and others, and is forthcoming in *Anthropocene* and *Honey Literary.* You can find her on Twitter at @kimmonjoo.

Daniel W.K. Lee is a third-generation refugee, queer, Cantonese American born in Kuching, Malaysia. He earned his MFA in Creative Writing at The New School, and his debut collection of poetry, *Anatomy of Want*, was published by QueerMojo/Rebel Satori Press. Daniel lives in New Orleans with the head-turning whippet Camden. Find out more about him at danielwklee.com

Rachel Kuanneng Lee writes poetry. Her work appears or is forthcoming at *Quarterly Literary Review Singapore, wildness, carte blanche, Dialogist, ANMLY, Sweet,* and elsewhere. She was a part of the inaugural cohort for the Brooklyn Poets Mentorship Program and is a Brooklyn Poets Fellow. You can reach her at rachel-lee.me.

Daryl Lim Wei Jie is a poet, translator and literary critic from Singapore. His latest collection of poetry is *Anything But Human* (2021), which was shortlisted for the 2022 Singapore Literature Prize. His work has been featured in *Poetry Magazine, Poetry Daily,* and *The Southwest Review.* His poetry won the 2015 Golden Point Award, awarded by the National Arts Council, Singapore. He edited *Food Republic: A Singapore Literary Banquet* (2020), the first definitive anthology of literary food writing from Singapore. He is putting together an anthology of Malaysia-Singapore writing, *The Second Link.*

Susan L. Lin is a Taiwanese American storyteller who hails from southeast Texas and holds an MFA in Writing from California College of the Arts. Her novella *Goodbye to the Ocean* was the winner of the 2022 Etchings Press novella prize. More of her work can be found online at https://susanllin.wordpress.com/.

Gabriel Awuah Mainoo is a Ghanaian writer, poet, editor, and lyricist. Winner of the 2021 Africa Haiku Prize and the LFP/RML/Library of Africa and the African Diaspora chapbook prize, he is the author of five poetry books and the forthcoming *Sea Ballet.* His writings have appeared in *Wales Haiku Journal, EVENT, Prairie Fire,* and the *Best New African Poets* anthologies (2018, 2019, 2020).

Awadhendra dev Narayan was a poet and author from Gaya, Bihar, noted for his social critique through poetry. His works are marked by extraordinary intellectual reflection on common sentiments, keen observation of everyday human life, and profound insights into the dynamics of social psyche.

Ramil Niyazov-Adyldzhyan is a poet, artist, and translator. He is an alumnus of the Open Literature School of Almaty (poetry seminar by Pavel Bannikov) and an employee of the Krel Cultural Center; he graduated from the department of liberal arts and sciences of St. Petersburg State University. In 2019 he was longlisted for the Arkady Dragomoshchenko Prize. He is the editor of polutona.ru.

Chisom Charles Nnanna (he/him/his) is a Nigerian creative writer and student of mass communication in the University of Ilorin. He is the winner of the 13th edition of *Tush Magazine* Bi-monthly Writing Contest; the two-time winner of the Shuzia Poetry Contest; the top entrant of the Nigerian Students Poetry Prize, 2021; and the finalist of the Eriata Oribhabor Poetry Prize, 2020.

Asel Omar is a graduate of the Maxim Gorky Literature Institute in Moscow and a member of the Writers' Union of Kazakhstan. She is the author of four books of fiction, a collection of poetry, and numerous articles. Her long short story "Black Snow of December," about a popular political uprising in Almaty in 1986, caused great controversy at the time of its publication.

Kanat Omar graduated with a degree in film direction from the St. Petersburg State Cultural Academy in 1996. He has lived in Astana since 2001. His writing has been featured in journals and anthologies of Russian-language poetry from Kazakhstan and the international Russian-speaking world.

Rahad Abir is a writer from Bangladesh. His work has appeared or is forthcoming in *Prairie Schooner, The Los Angeles Review, The Bombay Literary Magazine, The Wire, Himal Southasian, Courrier International,* and elsewhere. He has an MFA from Boston University. He received the 2017-18 Charles Pick Fellowship at the University of East Anglia. Currently he is working on a short story collection, which was a finalist for the 2021 Miami Book Fair Emerging Writer Fellowship.

Purbasha Roy is a writer from Jharkhand, India. Her work has appeared or is forthcoming in *SIAMB!, Bluestem, DASH, VIEW!, Bayou Review, long con, Hive Avenue, Delicate Friend,* and elsewhere.

Dr. Shalini Sengupta earned her PhD from the University of Sussex and is a Ledbury Poetry Critic. Her research specialisms are in modern and contemporary writing; twentieth- and twenty-first-century women's writing; and avant-garde poetry. Her academic and public-facing work has appeared in or is forthcoming from *Modernism/modernity, Journal of British and Irish Innovative Poetry, Contemporary Women's Writing,* Poetry Book Society, *Poetry Wales,* and *harana poetry.*

Sebastian Taylor has an undergraduate degree in physics from the University of St Andrews and is now pursuing an MLitt in curatorial practice at the Glasgow School of Art. They are fascinated by performance poetry, and they write on the themes of queering the body, self, and space, after having served as the head editor of the university's creative writing society.

Kevin Tsai, originally from Taiwan, received his PhD in comparative literature from Princeton University. His research interests include Roman poetry, Tang Dynasty narrative, translation studies, and contemporary film. He is Professor of Chinese at the University of South Alabama, and his best friend is really great at following "sit" and "stay" in English and German.

Avinash Chandra Vidyarthi was a Bhojpuri author and poet, born in 1928 in Shahpur, Arrah in Bihar. His works include the short story publication 'Daga Baji Gail', the poetry collection 'Anasail Raag', and the satirical essay 'Beta ke Naihar'. Although he was a prolific writer in terms of employment of a variety of forms, he was particularly distinguished in the comical satire subgenre of Bhojpuri literature. He was also one of the editors of *Bhikhari Thakur Rachnavali,* a compilation of the works of the celebrated Bhojpuri folk writer, poet, and playwright Bhikhari Thakur.

Lydia Wei is a junior at Stanford University. Her poems appear or are forthcoming in *The Adroit Journal, DIAGRAM, wildness, The Margins: Asian American Writers' Workshop, harana poetry,* and elsewhere. She lives in Gaithersburg, Maryland. She likes blackberries and cherries and very long walks.

Jackson Minjoon Wright is an aspiring poet and musician living in the Northern California Bay Area. A Korean American adoptee raised in Kansas City, he writes about the particularities of adoption and secluded life in the Midwest. Heartily inspired by poets such as Aimee Nezhukumatathil, he hopes to take a tender look at the harmful events that come to pass and shine a celebratory light on the wonderful moments that can often feel fleeting and revelatory. In his downtime, he works at a publishing house and writes music.

Katherine E. Young is the author of the poetry collections *Woman Drinking Absinthe* and *Day of the Border Guards* and the editor of *Written in Arlington.* She is the translator of *Look at Him* (Anna Starobinets) and *Farewell, Aylis* (Akram Aylisli). Her translations of contemporary Russian-language poetry have won international awards; she was named a 2017 National Endowment for the Arts translation fellow. From 2016 to 2018, she served as the inaugural Poet Laureate for Arlington, Virginia. https://katherine-young-poet.com/

ABOUT GAUDY BOY

From the Latin *gaudium*, meaning "joy," Gaudy Boy publishes books that delight readers with the various powers of art. The name is taken from the poem "Gaudy Turnout," by Singaporean poet Arthur Yap, about his time abroad in Leeds, the United Kingdom. Similarly inspired by such diasporic wanderings and migrations, Gaudy Boy brings literary works by authors of Asian heritage to the attention of an American audience and beyond. Established in 2018 as the imprint of the New York City–based literary nonprofit Singapore Unbound, we publish poetry, fiction, and literary nonfiction. Visit our website at www.singaporeunbound.org/gaudyboy.

Winners of the Gaudy Boy Poetry Book Prize

Waking Up to the Pattern Left By a Snail Overnight, by Jim Pascual Agustin

Time Regime, by Jhani Randhawa

Object Permanence, by Nica Bengzon

Play for Time, by Paula Mendoza

Autobiography of Horse, by Jenifer Sang Eun Park

The Experiment of the Tropics, by Lawrence Lacambra Ypil

Poetry

New Singapore Poetries, edited by Marylyn Tan and Jee Leong Koh

Fiction and Nonfiction

Picking off new shoots will not stop the spring, edited by Ko Ko Thett and Brian Haman

The Infinite Library and Other Stories, by Victor Fernando R. Ocampo

The Sweetest Fruits, by Monique Truong

And the Walls Come Crumbling Down, by Tania De Rozario

The Foley Artist, by Ricco Villanueva Siasoco

Malay Sketches, by Alfian Sa'at

From Gaudy Boy Translates

Amanat, edited by Zaure Batayeva and Shelley Fairweather-Vega

Ulirát, edited by Tilde Acuña, John Bengan, Daryll Delgado, Amado Anthony G. Mendoza III, and Kristine Ong Muslim